John Cheshire, Medical Consultant at Thickers Hospital, was warded. He was delirious, perhaps dying.

.   .   .   .   .

It was on the morning after the hospital dance that Cheshire was discovered missing. Also missing was Val Ridgeway, one of the student nurses. A mysterious voice on the telephone led Cheshire's Houseman, Sam, and young Nurse Brown, to the rescue. What followed was nightmare. For Sam was engaged to Val; and, although the Grape Vine linked "Brownie's" name with that of young Doctor Stead, she had found John Cheshire strangely disturbing.

Also by HILARY NEAL

FACTORY NURSE
STAR PATIENT
LOVE LETTER

and published by CORGI BOOKS

HILARY NEAL

HOUSEMAN'S SISTER

TRANSWORLD PUBLISHERS
LONDON

HOUSEMAN'S SISTER

A CORGI BOOK

Originally published in Great Britain
by Mills & Boon Ltd.

PRINTING HISTORY

Mills & Boon Edition published 1964
Corgi Edition published 1964

Corgi Books are published by Transworld Publishers, Ltd.,
Park Royal Road, London, N.W.10

Made and printed in Great Britain by
Richard Clay and Company, Ltd., Bungay, Suffolk

HOUSEMAN'S SISTER

CHAPTER ONE

WHEN I was six I burned to become a nurse. Someone gave me a Little Nurse set for Christmas—a cap and apron printed with large red crosses, a plastic thermometer and a round tin badge reading LITTLE HOME NURSE—and all my dolls were permanently bedridden, and had laryngeal perforations where I had stuck the thermometer. My brother Sam, who was nine and scorned women's ploys, planned to be a marine explorer. He proposed to zoom about the seabed in a contraption he had just invented called Brown's Bathybung—a sort of portable submarine prefab—in which he would muse in solitude safe from feminine distraction, eventually surfacing to win a Nobel prize for geophysics.

Now I am a nurse and Sam is a doctor. This is fine. I accept it. The world is a large place dotted with thousands of hospitals, and there ought to be room for both of us. But one morning last autumn I collided with Sam in the Bunny Run and realised that I had been a little over-optimistic about this.

The Bunny Run is a long narrow corridor connecting all the ward blocks and bisecting them into male and female halves. It runs parallel to what is known as the Main Drag, a wide, polished promenade decked with pot plants, linking ward blocks along one side with departments and offices along the other. Obviously nobody in her senses uses the Main Drag much, because it is always littered with Admin types looking for trouble, and stridden by lordly consultants smelling of after-shave lotion and not looking where they are going. So most of the to-ing and fro-ing at Thickers—as most people call Thickbroom Hall Hospital—takes place in the Bunny Run. The surgical end gets pretty cluttered

7

with extra traffic on operating days, so the medical end is where people tend to stand and talk, and this makes the whole length fairly hazardous to negotiate at speed. Especially when carrying anything, as one so often is.

I was heading for the path. lab. with a tray of specimens in test-tubes and jars when I hit Sam. The specimens rocked and then settled, but it was rather a nasty moment, so I said, "You crackpot! Can't you look where you're going?" before I performed a sort of double-take and added, "Sam! It *can't* be you." Ever since Sam had qualified he had been hounding down resident appointments at London hospitals, because he said the provinces were overcrowded with red-brick graduates with unbounded determination and picturesque unmedical accents, and London would offer more scope. So it was something of a shock to meet him, wearing a white houseman's jacket, in the Bunny Run at Thickers, bang in the top right-hand isthmus of unmetropolitan Warwickshire.

"It can be, and it is," he said, looking as superior as all junior housemen do in the beginning, before we second-years have trained them. He twisted his head to read the label on my tray. "And if you're really working on Ward Seven you'll very soon know it. I'm Dr. Cheshire's new H.P."

This was going to be a crushing blow to my friend Val Ringway. For weeks she had been looking forward to the day when Miss Woolley, Dr. Cheshire's current house physician, would take herself off and leave a vacancy for some attractive male sufficiently lowly to fraternise with mere pros. And now, instead of the tall, dark, wistful heart-throb she had been conjuring up, here was Sam. Tall and dark, certainly, like me. But that was about all. I said: "Poor old Val. She was hoping for some kind of Kildare this time. You anti-hero, you!" Then I remembered why I was in a hurry. "Heavens, it's rounds in ten minutes' time, and I haven't put out the sphyg. and things yet. Stand aside if you don't want your nice new jacket ruined."

I began to thread my way rapidly through the nurses and

housemen, and porters, and dressing-gowned patients in wheelchairs, and ward sisters prowling their way back from the office, and reached the turning for the path. lab. before the edge of the tray caught anyone else. This time it was Dr. Cheshire himself, and it was he, not I, who steadied the tottering jars. He shook his head at me gently and murmured: "Nurse Brown, that is not the way to carry a tray safely. Allow me." He took the tray from me, laid it along one forearm and gripped it with the other hand. "Like that. Have you never watched experienced waiters?"

If it had not been purely a rhetorical question I could have explained that I normally frequented self-service coffee bars and that my experience of observing waiters was limited to watching Ernest, at the chicken restaurant down the road, tearing about with plates piled in threes like bedpans. "Yes, sir," I said meekly. One has to speak meekly to consultants, whatever provocation they may offer, because they are very important people in the hospital hierarchy, and a pro is the lowest form of life—except of course for junior housemen. In fact, very few consultants ever have occasion to address pros at all except through third and fourth parties. Dr. Cheshire was one of the few; partly because he was newly appointed and could still remember being an R.M.O., and partly because he was Australian and therefore less of a devoté to English medical etiquette than most people, though he could lay it on with the best of them if he had to.

He put the tray on my arm and nodded. "Well, rounds," he said. "I appear to have no registrar this morning, and no H.P., but no doubt Sister Mumby is expecting me?" He ambled away along the corridor, and this was unusual, because he had long legs and was reputed to have done a four-minute mile in his final year at the University. I imagined he was giving Mr. Franks, his registrar, time to find him. Mr. Franks and Sam ought to have been at the ready in the front hall when he arrived, and any other consultant would have been distinctly chilly if he had entered ungreeted by his reception committee. Also any other consultant would have scorned to use the Bunny Run, and would have made his way to the wards along the Main Drag and not got involved with nurses carrying specimens. No doubt that was where Mr. Franks was looking for him.

I dumped the specimens on the enamel-topped table in the path. lab. lobby and ran back to the ward. Running is strictly forbidden at any hospital except in case of dire emergency, and Matron at Thickers has been known to cancel late passes on account of it, but with Dr. Cheshire due for rounds and only Sister and Staff Horrocks on the ward it seemed the lesser evil. Nobody arrested my flight, and when I steamed round the corner into Ward 7's female side Dr. Cheshire was still standing in the corridor outside the swing doors doing something intricate to one of his fingernails. Sam hovered at his elbow with a blank-sheeted clipboard under his arm, searching the horizon anxiously for Mr. Franks.

Mr. Franks was already in the ward, talking to Sister Mumby in her office, so when I had darted to the cupboard and got out the sphyg. and the ophthalmoscope, the patella hammer and the jar of spatulas, which it was my job to carry round after the retinue, I went back to the corridor and said: "If you're looking for Mr. Franks, sir, he's with Sister." Then I put my head round the office door and said, "Dr. Cheshire's here, Sister," and stood aside for her to plunge out. Sister Mumby plunges everywhere because she is large and loosely put together and congenitally incapable of doing anything sedately. So she plunges about, rather like a plump Welsh cob, whereas Staff Horrocks, who is bony and irritable, tends to make a series of darts along straight lines, tacking and gibing unpredictably at points where she suddenly thinks of things and alters her trajectory. What with one plunging and the other darting, and neither thinking along the same beam at any given moment in time, it is quite miraculous that they never actually collide, rather like the horses crossing over in the middle of the musical ride at the Tattoo.

Sister said, "Goodness! Thank you, Nurse," and flung herself out, putting her cuffs on as she went. Mr. Franks, looking pained, followed her, and both of them joined Dr. Cheshire, closing around him like escorts to the Colour as he entered the ward. Sam retreated to the background until I elbowed him out of my way and hissed at him to get on Mr. Franks's tail and stay there until he was spoken to. Staff Horrocks shot up the ward from the annexe, went off at sixty degrees to tug a bedspread straight and then aimed herself accurately at the square foot of space behind Sister.

Dr. Cheshire smiled patiently. "Well," he said. "Now that we are all assembled, let us proceed." He might as well have said: "Are you sitting comfortably? Then I'll begin." It was the same tone of voice. All his rounds are apt to begin in that key, but as he continues along the row of beds he concentrates keenly on what he is doing and is apt to hold out his hand for this and that without even speaking. So when, at the third bed, he looked fixedly at Mrs. May-cock's exposed legs and merely turned his hand palm upwards on the drawsheet, I leaned over the bottom rail and slapped the handle of the patella hammer into it. This is a peremptory habit that I picked up in the theatre, where if you don't slap instruments hard into gloved hands people either drop them or don't know they are there. Dr. Cheshire winced, came out of his trance and said: "Wow!" Then he blinked at me absently and added: "Thank you, Nurse."

When he had lifted Mrs. Maycock's bluish-white legs in turn and checked her reflexes he spun the rubber-edged hammer back at me in silence, and I replaced it on my tray. Then he straightened up, pulled his bottom lip and grunted, scanning the chart Staff Horrocks was holding at the ready. I opened up the sphyg. box and moved in, quite sure that he wanted to see Mrs. Maycock's blood-pressure vacillations for himself, but he looked at me, smiled suddenly straight into my face and said: "Wrong guess.

Spatula, please." It was the first time I had misread the signs, and it was annoying to see Sam grinning.

By standing well back in the middle of the ward as the procession moved on I could look through the glass entrance doors straight across the Bunny Run to our male ward. I could see Val Ringway across there watching me. When she realised she had caught my eye she made gestures to say she was going to first break and to ask whether I was. I let go of my tray with one hand and gestured back, conveying in what I felt was graphic mime that since Pro 4 had the morning off, Pro 3 had still not returned from the dispensary and Pro 1 had a lecture, I had no idea when, if ever, I should get across to the canteen.

Staff Horrocks said sharply: "Nurse! Throat swab."

Obviously this communiqué was already on its fourth repeat, having come from Dr. Cheshire to Mr. Franks, from Mr. Franks to Sister, from her to Staff Horrocks and from Staff to me. I blushed with shame and poked two throat-swab test-tubes at Sam, who was standing between me and Dr. Cheshire. Then I remembered to offer the spatula jar as well, and to pass Staff Horrocks a kidney dish to collect the débris with.

When we moved on again I was relieved to see Kerry Luck, our Pro 3, come bundling in carrying the heavy dispensary basket. When she had put it in the duty-room she came on down the ward on tiptoe and murmured: "I've been to coffee, if you want to go."

I raised my eyebrows at Staff Horrocks, she nudged Sister's elbow, and eventually a brief nod came back to me. I pushed the diagnostic tray at Nurse Luck and wondered why she was staring at my bare forearms. "Over to you," I said. "I'm off." In the kitchen, fishing my cuffs out of the bottom drawer, I got the message. I'd not only slipped up as an acolyte, I'd also committed the enormity of attending at rounds with my sleeves rolled up and no cuffs on.

It was all Sam's fault, of course. I told Val Ringway so in the canteen two minutes later. She said: "What are you in such a flap about? Is the Big Cheese in one of his tizzies?"

"No," I said. "But the new houseman's arrived and it put me off my stroke."

"What's he like?" Val's eyes lit up at once, turning from a kind of sultry hazel to the green with gold flecks that they are when she opens them wide and is on the alert. "Tell me, this minute! I've been living for the day."

It seemed a pity to say that the new H.P. was only my brother Sam, and not in the least the dreamboat she had been waiting for during Miss Woolley's occupation, so I said: "Not bad. Not at all bad. Tall, dark, brown eyes. Nice voice. A bit uppity, but aren't they all at first?"

"Did he tell you his name?" She bit into a gingernut enthusiastically, and hung on my words.

"No, he didn't." It was true enough: he hadn't.

"Never mind, we'll soon know." She swallowed the rest of her biscuit and stood up. "My dear, I must get back before they come over to male side."

"Relax." Over her shoulder I saw Dr. Cheshire and Sam coming into the canteen. "They're here. Having a break now, evidently."

Without turning round, Val said excitedly: "Where are they? Are they coming this way?"

One of the nice things about Thickers is that we have this very democratic canteen, which everyone uses regardless of rank. At proper mealtimes, of course, we go to our dining-room over in the Home and the residents go to theirs, but for between-time snacks we all use the canteen because it is close to the wards, half-way along the Main Drag. But though it is used by practically everyone from consultants to raw cap-conscious Lambs from the P.T.S., people don't often mix *ad lib*. The various strata of hospital society tend to separate out and to overlap only at the edges. That's to say consultants and Admin sisters will hobnob with registrars and ward sisters; they in their turn are not unlikely to share tables with Staff Nurses and senior housemen, who have been known to tolerate the company of junior men and senior pros. For the most junior pros of all the only male company to be had is normally that of lab. or theatre technicians or of the occasional fifth-year student, since Thickers isn't a teaching hospital and students usually come only sporadically to look at specific cases recommended by their professors. Some of the keen types come voluntarily, too, to help in Casualty and learn aseptic techniques where there is less competition than there is in their teaching hospitals. It was therefore something of an embarrassment when Sam, who clearly knew no better, brought two cups of coffee to our table and pulled back one of the chairs for Dr. Cheshire.

Val shot a good look at Sam, said, "Good morning, sir," to Dr. Cheshire and bolted, leaving me feeling like a circus usherette who has wandered into the lion's cage by mistake. Because it was quite as public as that, with the canteen packed to capacity, and the girls at the next table raising their eyebrows at me.

I tried to swallow the hot coffee quickly and choked. When I had finished mopping my eyes Dr. Cheshire said: "You don't mind if we join you, Nurse? All the other tables seem to be full."

"Of course not, sir." I put my handkerchief away. "It's a busy time."

"Yes. Normally I come later, but I'm waiting for some lab. reports before I finish my round."

"The path. lab., Nurse," Sam elaborated meaningly.

"The specimens were a bit late going down," I said, feeling guilty, quite unable to explain that it wasn't my fault but that of the junior night nurse, who had gone gaily off duty leaving the whole batch in the sluiceroom.

"So I recall," Dr. Cheshire said. He looked amused rather than angry, though it isn't always easy to tell what he is thinking because he has a thin, rather expressionless face, which only comes to life when he smiles. When he does he looks at least ten years younger, because he has fair hair that would wave if he didn't flatten it down, and eyes rather like Val's which change colour according to the light they are seen in. They were a kind of translucent opal blue at that moment, so I judged he was not unduly put out. "I'm afraid I added to the delay by demonstrating to Nurse the proper method of carrying a loaded tray."

Sam pinched my knee under the table, and I reacted with a suppressed squeak. Dr. Cheshire frowned into his coffee cup and asked: "Well, Brown? Are you getting the picture? Do you know your way about yet?"

That struck me as a double-edged remark to say the least, but Sam took it at its face value. "Not yet, sir. I haven't really had time to explore."

"No?" I was sure he was still teasing. "Well, we must remedy that. When you've written up your notes you must make the grand tour. The ward plan's simple enough to master, but the old building, the Nurses' Home and so on, is a regular warren. Isn't it, Nurse?"

There was nothing in the old building—the original Thickbroom Hall, which had once been a stately home—to interest Sam, and he knew it. Matron's flat, the R.M.O.'s and R.S.O.'s quarters, the boardroom and our dining-room, and the two wings given over to nurses' bedrooms were not usually penetrated by housemen.

"Yes, sir," I agreed. "It will be nice when they finish the building programme. The night nurses have lived over the stables long enough."

"Over the *stables*? That sounds remarkably unsavoury!"

"Not really, sir. Rather like—well, mews flats. Only there's no heating system."

"And you'll be going on nights during the cold weather?"

"I expect so, sir."

"We must make a note of that, too, Brown," he told Sam, whose head was bent studiously over his clipboard. "Heating for the night nurses' quarters!"

The conversation was getting dangerously familiar and unethical, and I could see Staff Horrocks at the counter looking at us over her uplifted nose like a pointer scenting game. I excused myself and hurried out.

It was quite the longest conversation I had ever had with a consultant, and I thought about it off and on for the rest of the morning as I worked my way through my list of blanket-baths and helped to serve the patients' lunch.

I was off duty at two o'clock, so I automatically went to second lunch at one-thirty after tidying the ward, and told Staff Horrocks, as I put my cuffs on: "It's my afternoon, Staff. Need I come back at two?"

"No, Nurse. You can go off. And when you come back at five I hope you'll do a little less daydreaming. Really, I can't think what came over you this morning!" She sniffed. "If you're going to be fluttered by the presence of a new houseman . . ."

It occurred to me that because of the interruption of our coffee break I had still not explained to Val that Sam was my brother. I decided it would do no harm to string her along for a little while before I broke the news. So when she leaned across the lunch table and said: "Isn't he a poppet?" I agreed.

"Yes, he certainly has something," I admitted. "He's *different*."

Val gave me one of her looks. "Now listen, Brownie, no poaching. You've got your little friend in Casualty, to say nothing of Simon James, so kindly lay off!" She sounded exactly the way she had in the fourth form when I'd gone to the school play at the boys' school next door with a scrum-half she had had her eye on for two whole terms.

I giggled. She was rising beautifully. "My little friend in Casualty? I like that. Peter's fourteen stone if he's an ounce. Anyhow, he isn't *my* friend: if you ask me he divides his favours pretty evenly. . . . As for Simon James, how often do we see him? He hasn't been near the place since he came down to watch Mr. Holtby do that kidney graft." I sighed appreciatively. "No, I think the new man will be very use-ful. He'll fill a long-felt need."

"Then it's war?"

"War to the death," I said. "In fact, I'm pretty sure it'll be his half day tomorrow, and——"

"But it's ours, too. You said we'd go to Rackhams to look at the parkas. Surely you're not going to back out *now*?"

Outside the dining-room I said: "Come to the phone-box with me."

"Who are you going to ring?"

I looked mysterious, and her curiosity brought her with me. She squashed into the box beside me as I picked up the receiver. When the switchboard answered, instead of asking for an outside line through the coinbox, I said in the deepest voice I could manage: "Get me Dr. Cheshire's H.P., please."

Val goggled. "You're *not* going to *ring* him?" She was quite horrified.

"Why not? I dare say he's lonely, coming to a strange place. . . . You don't get anywhere by being shy, my dear."

I had never seen her so agitated. "You must be crazy!" she hissed. "Put it down, quickly, before they find him."

I fended her off. "Hallo? Is that Dr. Cheshire's H.P.? This is Nurse Brown, Ward Seven."

"Oh. It's you," Sam said. "Fetching me from my lunch . . . What gives?"

I looked sidelong at Val and made appreciative faces, rolling my eyes with delight. "I—well, I wondered what you were doing with your half day tomorrow, actually."

"Ah, there you can help me. Any nice little blondes avail-able? I was thinking of the ice rink, given suitable com-pany."

"The ice rink?" I made more faces at Val. She was crimson with fury. Also she is a much better skater than I am. "Hm, yes, I think it could be managed."

"You'd better come too, and bring another chap," he suggested. "Just in case your candidate proves heavy in hand. Are you free?"

"Yes," I agreed. "I can bring my friend. Who else had you thought of? . . . Peter Stead? What a good idea !"

"Who the something is Peter Stead?" Sam wanted to know.

"Yes, well you ask him then," I pressed on. "You'll see him at dinner, won't you?"

"Oh? Will I?"

"That'll be lovely. 'Bye for now. Oh—— What time?"

"You tell me."

"Threeish, yes. Yes, we can manage that. Outside the main gate? Oh—just one thing. I'd rather you didn't tell anyone about our . . . our relationship. You know how people talk."

"Don't worry. I haven't," Sam said. "Who'd brag about having you for a sister?"

Val nearly exploded when I put the receiver down. She wasn't interested in Peter Stead, she said, and what did I think I was playing at? Really, I was the end. She didn't know how I had the face to ring him at all. In fact, she had a good mind not to turn up. And so on. "Anyhow, he's sure to latch on to me," she said complacently when she had calmed down. "Dark men never like dark women. And you know you dote on Peter."

In fact, it didn't work out that way at all. Sam, who is not as slow in the uptake as he pretends to be, made a dive for me when we assembled next afternoon, and left Peter to deal with Val. We were going in Peter's car, he said, and we had to walk round the Hall to the residents' car park. He clutched my elbow and hurried me on ahead of the other two. I saw Matron's surprised face as we took a short cut across the lawn under her sitting-room window. "Now you've done it," I said. "I shall probably be flung in the foc's'le for that. Don't you *know* you're not allowed on the grass?"

"Never mind that. What's the set-up?"

"I'm merely ragging Val," I said. "After a suitable interval we'll let her snatch you from under my very nose, as it were. But keep it up for a bit, because Peter bores her stiff. Then she'll be all the gladder when you sit up and take notice."

He grinned. "I am with you, sister mine. I must say she's not bad looking."

"She's an extremely nice girl, as a matter of fact. I've done you proud. So no hankypanky. You haven't told Peter our shameful secret, have you?"

"Of course not. You asked me not to. . . . Anyway, it's more fun to keep it quiet, isn't it? We might both want an alibi sometime. An out, as the dear Americans say."

We kept it going beautifully, all the way to the ice rink. We sat in the back of Peter's dilapidated saloon, holding hands just obviously enough for Val to notice and looking madly innocent every time she turned round, which was pretty often. By the time we got to the rink it was "Blackie" and "Brownie" and there was no question about who paid for whom at the pay-box.

Once we were on the ice Peter, clearly bored, went off on a circuit of his own, and Val promptly developed bootlace trouble. I glared at her when she asked Sam to fix it for her. And when they went off arm in arm I made my way to Peter looking suitably disconsolate. Val's triumphant smile as she hurtled past with Sam was well worth all the machinations.

Peter said: "It's a waltz, now. Come on." Waltzing with Peter was a thing I had always found exciting, and on ice it was wonderful. Consequently we didn't talk until the radiogram went off. Then he said: "I've been admiring the amateur theatricals. He's your brother, isn't he?"

I opened my eyes wide. "Is that what he told you?"

"No. But you've got the same nose, as well as the same name. And you'd never have brought Val Ringway along for *me*. Q.E.D. . . . Correct?"

"There's clever," I said admiringly, in a Welsh accent.

"Only don't tell her. Let her have her glow. It's good for her morale. Boosts her ego."

Peter looked surprised. "Does it need boosting?"

"In fact, yes." I looked round the ice to make sure the other two were out of earshot. They were. They were at a standstill, talking their heads off, at the other end of the rink. "Yes. That's the point. You remember Jock Marston?"

"Yes. The chap Miss Cardigan replaced last month, you mean? Didn't stay long, did he?"

"Miss Woolley," I said. "You nearly had *me* calling her Miss Cardigan the other week. And somebody kidded our junior pro that her name was Miss Lamb, and she——"

"What did the Cardigan say?"

"Turned pink and said: 'Don't be impudent, Nurse!' Poor old Apsley-Hunter."

"Poor old *what*?"

"Apsley-Hunter. Robinia Apsley-Hunter. A flower of the local cashocracy, my dear. Isn't her papa on the Board?"

"Ah, so he is. Very higgerant, very rich."

"Quite. Dear Robinia isn't exactly higgerant. She's really rather pathetic. She was thrown into this squalid profession straight from some Swiss finishing school, and what she knows about perfectly ordinary things like cutting b. and b., or cleaning sinks, would go on a postage stamp."

"Anyhow, what about Jock Marston? You were saying . . .?"

"I was saying that he's why Val's morale needs solidifying."

"Oh? I thought I knew all about all the internal romances. I certainly missed that one."

I nodded. "Yes. It was very short, very sweet and very undermining, I gather. Just between you and me, of course."

"Of course." Peter squeezed my hand in warning, because we were swooping past the other two. Then he said: "Go on." He didn't release my hand, though, and it was very pleasant.

"That's all, really. Except that she took it pretty hard.

And when he went off in the middle of his time it knocked her for six. . . . Why did he, Peter?"

"I don't really know. He's at the Queen's now, anyway. Doing H.S. to the ophthalmic bloke. Near enough to call at Thickers if he wanted to."

"She doesn't know that. Maybe it's as well. Anyhow, it'll do her good to think she's brought off a snatch, as it were. Convince her that she still has what it takes. Sam will probably fall for her. He's very susceptible to small fair girls."

"I go for tall dark ones myself," Peter murmured. I didn't take it too seriously. The big trouble with Peter had always been that he was the complete chameleon. Then he said: "Sam? Sam Brown. Ah, that explains it."

"Explains what?"

"Why he told us his nickname was Belter."

"And that brings it full circle," I said. "The only reason he's always been called Sam—because his name's really Durham—is because when he was little he was swaggering about in Father's Sam Browne harness, and Father began calling him Sam, and it stuck." I looked at Sam's mischievous face as we passed them again—Val was having the time of her life—and said: "Imagine calling him Durham! It just wouldn't suit him at all."

"You once told me that Peter didn't suit me."

"No more it does. A fine rock you are for a girl to cling to. A pebble in every ward, that's you."

He looked down at me—and a man has to be pretty tall to do that—in a way that he must have known perfectly well did odd things to my knees, so that I nearly stumbled as he whirled me round the corner of the rink. "There's an awfully big boulder in Ward Seven," he said. "I wonder Sister Mumby doesn't trip over it, the way she goes charging about the place."

I ignored that. "It's time we teamed up again," I suggested. "It won't give her a kick if it's too easy. I must go and make a few more eyes at my little brother."

"Little? I thought maybe you were unidentical twins."

"Don't tell Sam that! He's three years older than I am. Not that you'd think it, I agree. He's even more irresponsible than I am."

I chased Sam, one way and another, just enough to make Val feel slightly insecure, and then Peter suggested, as though I had bored him stiff: "Why don't we all go somewhere for a meal? There's time to drive out somewhere. And we've all just been paid."

"I haven't," Sam said indignantly. And then, forgetting his role momentarily, he took my handbag from me, poked through it and said: "Lend me three, there's a honey."

I snatched it back. "Really!" I said. "What is it about new housemen? Every batch we get is saucier than the last. It's very odd; when they're fifth-years they're so terribly earnest, all practising their bedside manners and cultivating sonorous voices against the day when they're consultants. And the instant they qualify they behave like fourth-formers. No, I *won't* lend you money. You shouldn't invite girls out if you can't afford it."

Val looked as though she was opening her mouth to offer a loan, and then Peter said: "All right, old man. I can set you up." He handed over a five-pound note. "See you on payday." It was very trusting of him.

I made a belated play to get into the back of the car with Sam and let Val beat me to it. Then I shrugged at her and got into the front with Peter. The gear lever in Peter's car is hard up against the passenger seat, and he managed to brush my shin several times in the course of changing gear. When I moved away he murmured, "Don't be like that," and glanced in the mirror. "Take a lesson from Sam," he said.

After a while I looked round. I needn't have been so furtive about it, because neither of them would have noticed. They were too busy looking at one another. In fact, Sam was wearing one of the sloppiest expressions I had even seen on his face. I was rather surprised. Sam had always been a great one for the girls, but he had usually managed to bend without falling. It seemed to me that Val was having a walk-over, and that was not exactly what I had planned. She needed to fight and win. It didn't occur to me then that she might have to, in earnest, later on.

Peter pulled in at a place I'd never heard of, and which looked like a cross between Haddon Hall and the Coal Board. Another Thickbroom Hall, in fact. "Home from home," I said. There were some extremely lush cars in the car park. "Only more so."

"Much more so. It's the top of the pops, foodwise, at the moment. The Old Curdworth Country Club, to give it its full title."

"You've been before then?"

"A couple of times." He looked round as he pulled on the handbrake. "Are you two with us, or do we leave you to daydream?"

When we got out I took Sam's arm possessively. "I'm starving," I said. "Lead me to it."

He tried to shake me off, and then capitulated when I pinched him. We marched through the panelled hall and into the restaurant. Val trailed behind, and Peter, left to lock up the car, came last. In that order we followed the head waiter, and when we sat down I deliberately wriggled my chair nearer to Sam's. "Darling," I said in a high bright voice. "Darling, I could eat a *horse*."

It was one of those moments. A split second before I opened my mouth the discreet orchestra under the balcony stopped playing. The people at the tables nearest to us fell silent simultaneously, and for some reason all the waiters stopped rattling cutlery, popping bottles and making things sizzle over their spirit lamps. Several heads turned our way before the background hum picked up again, and Sam said: "How will you have it? Poached Percheron? Soufflé of Suffolk Punch? Or just Shetland on toast?"

Val said: "Brownie, for goodness sake be quiet. Anybody would think you'd been drinking. And you can stop play-acting with Sam, because he's told me all about it."

"All about what?" I leaned forward. "Do tell."

Sam was capable of telling her almost anything: that he was my ex-husband, that he was working for M.I.5, or that he was the French Pretender. I would not have been surprised if she had thought he was the Minister of Health in disguise. But when she said, "About his being your brother," I was genuinely shocked.

I turned on him. "Sam, how could you? You surely didn't think Val was stupid enough to believe you, did you? She's not dim, you know. . . . I'll tell you the truth, now, Val. I was trying to protect you from it, but now you'd better know. He's the most unprincipled, dissolute——"

It was no use. They were both laughing.

"Well, you tried," Peter said. "Now let's eat." He waved over the waiter and began ordering competently. We left it to him—I because I knew he was aware of all my tastes, and Val and Sam because they weren't really interested in the food anyway.

I had been genuinely hungry before we began, but by the time I had fought my way through a prawn cocktail, steak Diane, sweet tomato ice—which sounded repulsive, but which was in fact delicious, though I chose it out of sheer perversity—and Gaelic coffee I felt I could never face food again.

When Sam got out of the car afterwards to take Val round to the Home I was still sitting drowsily in front with Peter, and not at all in a resistant frame of mind. Of course Peter kissed me, several times, and of course I loved it.

It is strange how delightful the most unproductive activities can be. For me to sit there kissing Peter Stead was about as much use as filling in a football coupon and then throwing it into the fire. Peter went out with all the girls; Peter was the most eligible male at Thickers; Peter knew it. But I still sat there making the most of my small share in him and wishing that I dare stay out late and climb in through the bathroom window the way some people did. But I never had any head for heights, and it wasn't worth the nervous stress of creeping past Home Sister's room. Other people get away with those things; I am always the one who is caught red-handed. I pulled myself out of his arms and said: "Peter, I must go. Anyhow, this is just a waste of time."

"I wouldn't say that." He opened the door for me. "And it wouldn't be the first time I'd created a diversion under Home Sister's window while somebody got in at the back."

He walked me out of the car park and round the building. I looked up at Home Sister's curtained window as we passed it. "What sort of diversion?"

"That you will discover when you stay out late."

"I see," I said. "Then I'll resign myself to permanent ignorance."

"You do everything the hard way, don't you, sweet?"

"Always," I said firmly. "It makes life safer and more interesting, both."

"Isn't that a contradiction in terms?"

"No. It isn't interesting to feel insecure. Not to me anyway." I thought of our junior pro on Ward 7. "Look at Apsley-Hunter," I said. "So insecure, and so dull."

"I shouldn't have thought she'd be either with half a million pounds in Daddy's stocking."

"You'll never be a psychiatrist, my dear."

"No," he said. "I don't aim to be. I aim to do surgery. I'm applying for a surgical registrarship."

This was new. "Oh? Which firm?"

"Lockyer's. . . . Here you are, delivered right to the door, and it still isn't bolted. Now you're safe you'd better have it interesting too, hadn't you?" When he let me go I ran all the way up to my room.

Val called in on the way back from the bathroom. She looked pretty starry-eyed. "Don't go overboard without your lifejacket," I warned her. "I mean, have your eyes open. He's a practised squire of dames, is our Sam."

"Yes? Well, his practising days are over. This is the

actual take," she said. She couldn't forget that her brother was a recording engineer. "Take One," she added. "And that's the one."

"Don't say I didn't warn you." I wiped off my smudged lipstick, looking in the mirror. "Who is Peter supposed to be taking out just now?"

"The last I heard was Staff Williams, from O.P." She looked at me hard. "Does it matter?"

"Not a bit," I assured her. "I was just curious. If his idea of a hot time in the old town tonight is to take Staff Williams out, he's very welcome. As far as I'm aware she's the complete iceberg. Alaskan Lullaby they called her at Queen's." It was not flattering, I felt, to be taken as an antidote.

"I'm seeing Sam again tomorrow night," she confided.

"You are? Well, there's a thing. *I* wasn't asked for a return fixture." It wasn't strictly true, of course. Peter had said he'd demonstrate his diversion tactics any time I cared to overstay my pass. But that wasn't quite the same thing. "You see? Gentlemen do prefer blondes."

"Peter doesn't. All his girls have been dark. Including you."

"You can include me out, as they say. I'm not a regular member of the harem. I'm just the good old stopgap, when Williams's icy mountains and Lawson's coral strand go sour on him. Temperate climate, that's me."

"You knew about Lawson, then? I was hoping you didn't."

That was really rather funny. Coralie Lawson was just about as notorious as it's possible for a nurse to be without its damaging her professional reputation. Because she was a spanking good theatre nurse, and well in line for a gold medal, she got away with murder where men were concerned. It simply wasn't possible for her to even stand and talk to one for more than two minutes without the jungle telegraph spreading the news. "Optimistic of you," I said. "When you take a girl like Lawson to a place like Queen's to a dance you don't expect it to be a well-kept secret for long. In fact, that's what I'd call publicity-seeking."

"I feel a heel," Val said. "I wish you felt the way I do about somebody." I didn't remind her that when she'd felt that way about Jock Marston I'd simultaneously been fighting the worst spell of Peter-fever I'd ever had. It had been a sort of malaria with me for months, coming back to hit me periodically until at last I'd developed an acquired immunity. I could take Peter or leave him alone, now. Or I was fairly sure I could.

"So do I," I said. I meant it, too.

"You know, all the time we were at school together I never knew you had a brother."

"I never knew about yours, either. After all, it's a long way from Hall Green to Walmley. I don't remember that we were ever on visiting terms. Let's face it, we weren't exactly bosom friends in those days, were we?"

"We certainly were not! Do you remember going to the boys' play with Keith Mackay? I could have strangled you."

"And I didn't even like him. It was just that he'd promised to teach me to play chess. Once he'd taught me I dropped him for somebody who'd teach me to skate." Most of my amours were strictly utilitarian in those days, I remembered. "Stanley somebody."

"Stanley Britton."

"That's the one. He was very good at skating and not at anything else that I ever discovered."

"Sam's a marvellous skater," Val mused. "Did Stanley teach him, too?"

I smiled. "No, I did."

Home Sister crackled into my room without warning, breathing noisily. "Do you know, Nurses, that your lights should have been out twelve minutes ago? And you haven't attempted to undress, even! I'll give you three minutes to get into bed. Now hurry. How *do* you expect to do your work if you don't have proper sleep? Come along, Nurse Ringway. Into your own room, please."

She wheezed off along the corridor and I heard her pitching into somebody else at the far end. That was the thing about Home Sister, she was a just beast. She nagged at all of us quite impartially, and if anyone was really in a spot she was there. She was as impartial, I reflected, as I turned out my light, as Peter Stead was with the girls.

CHAPTER TWO

In Ward 7-female it was Pro 2's responsibility to look after the four-hourly charts and treatments. So that if I went off at ten, or two, or six I had to run all these things in before I went. In practice, this meant that none of the four-hourly things was actually done at the nominal time but half an hour earlier, and since the night nurses pursued the same course, the object of the exercise was achieved. But Sister Mumby never could see this, and the earliest I dare begin—except on rounds days, which were a ritual unto themselves —was at ten minutes to the hour.

Next morning I was trying to deal with seven four-hourly temperatures, four four-hourly mouth cleanings, and a couple of sore backs which had to be turned, as well as the two-hourly feed for the query gastric ulcer. To do all these things properly in ten or twelve minutes is perfectly possible. But it does demand concentration and a quick trot. I was therefore not pleased when Sam, airily swinging his bright new stethoscope, came walking down the ward with the obvious intention of having a jolly little chat. He came up to me while I was cleaning the mouth of a poor old dear called Granny Waters, who was fortunately stone deaf, and said: "Thanks for the intro, mate." Sam spent his university vacations as a bus conductor—strictly for the adventure, as he said—and it still shows when he feels gay. "I couldn't have done better myself." He meant, I took it, that he approved of Val.

I moved on to the end bed, carrying the temperature tray now that all the mouths were done, and thrust a thermometer into Miss Pedler's mouth, already open for it. With her wrist in my hand and my watch out, I checked her respirations with half an eye while I found her pulse. Sam followed me. "For goodness sake scarper," I told him. "I'm busy." I began to count all over again.

"I only thought you'd like to know."

When I'd charted Miss Pedler I crossed the ward to Mrs. Maycock. Sam trailed after me. Then—as I'd known perfectly well she would—Sister Mumby came plunging down from the linen room with her keys jingling and her bosom heaving and said: "Now, young man! You haven't been house physician for two whole days, yet, and you've not yet learned rule number one, have you? Never, *never* distract the nurses from their work. I'll put up with towels on the floor, untidy writing on my clean charts and patients being examined without screens. But I will *not* have my nurses pestered, young man. Understood?"

"Pestered? Pestered, Sister?" Sam did his wide-eyed act.

"Pestered, I said. And pestered I meant. As for you, Nurse Brown, you're nearly in your third year. You'll soon be doing Pro 1, and finding yourself left in charge of the ward from time to time. You ought to know better. You're not a schoolgirl, to encourage every young man who wants to waste his time chattering to you!"

The net result of that little lot was that I didn't get over to the Home until a quarter-past ten, and my friend Hobbs, from O.P., had gone off for our weekly coffee session without me, thinking no doubt that I wasn't off, after all. By the time I ran her to earth at the chintzy café we used at that time she had the last person on earth with her—Coralie Lawson—and I couldn't possibly pump her about Staff Williams.

Lawson must have been between young men, or she would never have gone to the *Singing Kettle*, which was purely a feminine preserve. Unless, of course, she wanted to pump Hobbs about me, which was just a possibility. Certainly neither of us had anything to say in front of one another, and I spent most of the next quarter of an hour listening to the talk at the other tables, all of which were occupied by women. Women with loud voices and incredibly ugly but expensive hats, all looking exactly like outsize fur tea-cosies. The hats, not the women; although those in fur coats—and that type wears them all the year round—did rather resemble their own headgear. When I just sat quietly listening I realised what a din a few women can make, simply talking in twos and threes. It all seemed to be about absolutely nothing, except for a lot of name-dropping, but that didn't matter, because in fact they were all talking at once and listening only to themselves. And then I heard Lawson tell Hobbs: "Well, my dear, she was out with him last night, *and* he's bought two tickets for the October dance, so she must have something."

I wasn't fool enough to ask straight away, so I waited until she got up to go. She had absolutely nothing, as far as I could see, yet men found her fascinating. She wasn't even good-looking, though she took a lot of trouble with herself in small ways, keeping her eyebrows tidy, and putting grease on her eyelids, and all that kind of thing. Her hair was no-colour, but it was always severely neat, drawn back very smoothly from her blunt smooth face and high cheekbones. Hobbs was watching her, too, as she pulled her gloves on. She had a clinical way of doing this, as though they were rubber instead of kid. When she had said goodbye and walked out, very upright, Hobbs said: "Pure peasant, isn't she? Slav, or something. Short legs."

"More like an Eskimo," I suggested. "Slitty eyes. Not that she isn't a clinking theatre nurse. I mean, if I had to have a major op I'd as soon she was scrubbed up as not."

"Oh, me too," Hobbs agreed. "She's a perfectionist, you

see. She *has* to do everything perfectly because she can't face being wrong about anything."

"And *who* was out with him last night?" I said. "And *who* bought two tickets for the October dance? Not Peter Stead, for once, because I was with him myself."

Hobbs grinned. "I thought you might have been. Lawson was asking. I told her I hadn't a clue. . . . No, not Peter. The Big Cheese, actually."

"Dr. Cheshire?" I was startled. This really *was* new. "Truly?"

"I didn't know you cared!"

"I don't, you ass. But he's one of the few people around Thickers who's managed not to get himself talked about lately," I pointed out.

"He hasn't been here long enough, that's all. Three months is nothing."

"What about when he was R.M.O., two years ago?"

"Then," Hobbs said, "we were too young to care." How right she was.

"So, he was out last night. And not with Lawson. Well, that's in his favour anyhow. With whom?"

"You guess."

"I simply can't imagine. A sister, at least, I assume?"

"Well, obviously. Even he isn't unconventional enough to hobnob with anything less. Besides, he's not what I'd call attractive. Colourless, to my mind. He's hardly the type the youngsters go for, is he?"

"I wouldn't know," I said. "Was it Sister Branker?"

"From O.P.? Good heavens, no. She's heavily involved with somebody outside, we gather. Somebody who takes her to concerts in a Bentley, and sends flowers every Saturday. Corsages, I mean, not vase-flowers."

I had heard that one before. I had also heard an apocryphal story about one of the O.P. people finding a bill from the local Interflora depot, made out to Sister Branker, for six corsages at twelve and six a time. That I did not believe. Some people will say anything.

"Then was it somebody from medical, or surgical?"

"Medical."

Then I thought of Sister Thorpe, over in Ward 7-male. She is youngish—around thirty, I suppose—and very quiet. Rather a dark horse, really. She is well thought of as a ward sister—which means that she is fair and not a martinet—but nobody then had ever been sufficiently interested in her to speculate about her private life. "Sister Thorpe, then," I said. "Though if anyone's colourless, she is. Sepia right through."

"You never can tell with the quiet sort," Hobbs pondered. "Look at Lawson—she doesn't *look* a man-eater, does she? Yes, Thorpe. So now you have it."

I was dumbfounded. Not by the news that I had guessed correctly. Nor by the knowledge that Sister Thorpe did, after all, do something else besides looking at the television set in the sisters' sitting-room. Nor even by the fact that Dr. Cheshire was pursuing the sister on his male ward. None of these things was enough to rock me back on my heels. What did was the realisation that I minded very much that Dr. Cheshire might be in danger of making a fool of himself. If he got himself talked about, I thought, I should want to march across to the male ward and quietly eliminate Sister Thorpe, inoffensive though she might seem. "She'd better be careful," I said. "He isn't one of your fast-and-loose kind." Not, I meant, like Peter Stead. "He's the kind to take things hard."

"Rot. He's as tough as they come."

"Yes," I agreed. "But not that way. At least, I'm pretty sure he isn't."

I planned to ask Val when I saw her, to keep her eye on things across the other side of the Bunny Run.

In fact, I had the opportunity for a fresh look at Sister Thorpe myself during the afternoon. Staff Horrocks dragged me away from laying the tea trolley to go and borrow a drum of sterile towels. We don't use many on medical wards, so we don't have the same regular routine as the surgical side do of packing drums every day to go down to the autoclave. Therefore we're apt to run out of them from time to time, and have to borrow. Since every ward has its own drums, and loathes lending them out in case they are annexed permanently, it seemed more likely that I'd get a friendly reception on our own male ward than I would anywhere else. Sister Mumby was off, so Sister Thorpe would be on, and that decided me.

I went across the Bunny Run and through the glass doors of the male ward and tapped on the duty-room door. Instead of telling me to come in, as anyone else would have done, Sister Thorpe came to open the door and stood there as though it was the front door of a little house and I was a brush salesman. She is not a smiley type, but when she saw who it was she quite definitely smiled. Only it wasn't a smile of greeting, because she suppressed it at once and said: "Yes, Nurse?"

"Sister Mumby wondered whether you could spare a drum of towels, Sister."

"There's a half drum here you can take, Nurse." She pointed to the shelf beside her.

As I reached past her to get it I caught a distinct whiff of perfume. I even knew what it was, because I am rather addicted to hanging round the perfumery counter at Boots' and experimenting with dabs from all the test bottles on the stand. The reason I have this addiction—and the reason a lot of other nurses have it too—is that perfume is strictly forbidden when on duty. This in fact implies a total ban, because if we used it off duty there would be a carry-over into duty hours, so we never do use it, but satisfy our craving for something sweeter than Dettol by sniffing in chemists' shops. That is why I knew that Sister Thorpe had been anointing herself pretty freely with *Je Reviens*, which is one of my favourites. Too sweet for me, but lovely on other people. Anyhow, it wasn't my business, so I took the drum and went; but I did wonder why anyone as law-abiding as

Sister Thorpe would be wearing perfume at three o'clock in the afternoon when she couldn't have been out since the night before.

I said as much to Pirie, our Pro 1, when we had given out the teas. Pirie is completely without charm of any obvious kind, having a thin freckled face, ginger-brown hair and round glasses which somehow manage to be always slightly askew, even when she buys new ones. It could be that her nose, and not the glasses, is at fault. But she is nevertheless no fool and frequently comes out with penetrating remarks which indicate that she does a good deal of thinking, and observing too, in a quiet way. So as we momentarily stood idle against the radiator watching everyone mopping up sandwiches and Madeira cake, after we'd fed the lying-down patients, I said: "I went over to male side to borrow a drum, and Sister Thorpe's going about simply reeking of perfume."

Pirie pushed up her glasses and looked blankly out into the garden. "At this hour?"

"That's what I mean."

"If it's last night's hangover," she said, "and the half-life of perfume not being all that, then what did she smell like last night? And if it *isn't* last night's, what is she trying to prove?"

"That she's aware of herself as a woman, I suppose."

"She never has been before." She looked at me thoughtfully. "I know—it's the new H.P. He's stirred something in her."

"Never," I said. "If the gipsy in her hasn't been stirred by now I don't see it waking up for *him*."

"No? Oh. I thought you were slightly interested yourself."

"Not in that way," I said truthfully. "It's more of a sisterly feeling. Did you know that Sister Thorpe was out with Dr. Cheshire last night? Or so Lawson says."

"Ah, that explains it."

"Explains what?"

She began going round with the big pot pouring second cups, so I collected a few empty plates while she did it. When she came back she said: "Now I understand. Sister Mumby's gone out to have her hair set, and she never does. And Horrocks says *she's* going out with him tomorrow."

"Who—Horrocks?"

"No. Sister. That's why she's having her hair set."

"I don't believe you!"

"Oh, yes. It's true. Well that explains Sister Thorpe, doesn't it. Obviously it's just a duty thing. Both his ward sisters."

While we cleared the ward I was humming Crusader choruses to myself. I often do. They are sometimes very comforting in moments of stress, especially the ones like *"I can do all things . . ."* But the one I happened to be humming this time was: *"Joy, joy, joy."* Mrs. Maycock said: "You sound happy, Nurse."

"Yes, I am," I said. "Mark you, I don't know why, but there it is."

The woman in the next bed said: "It's that young fellow, that's what it is. Got his eye on her, I reckon."

If that was what they wanted to think they were welcome.

I didn't see Pirie again for a bit, because while I was doing evening cat-licks and making beds with Apsley-Hunter she was doing the medicines, since Staff Horrocks was tied up doing a linen inventory and it was Kerry Luck's half day. Apsley-Hunter is hardly the person I'd choose to make beds with, in fact I'd have been quicker on my own. She is thin and drooping, with one of those wispy fringes that make people look like Skye terriers who have just got up. She says it's a Bardot fringe and that everyone, but everyone, in France has one, which conjures up quite a picture. She never walks, she drifts, like a blown leaf. She is always leaning on something, too, and somehow managing to convey that she's an exhausted deb after a round of wild social whirling. In fact, she's always in bed by ten and never goes anywhere except the cinema.

At every bed I had to remind her: "Bring the chair, Nurse." And at every bed she would lean on the top rail making light conversation while I whipped the blankets off and on again and struggled to organise pillows with one hand and support the patient with the other. By the time we came to Miss Pedler, who is a bit on the Mrs. Battle scale, having "to her mighty frame a pinguitude withal", I had had enough of this. "For Pete's sake," I told her, "stop drooping about the place like a superannuated tulip and *do* something. Take Miss Pedler's other arm and help me to lug her up the bed."

Offendedly she linked her arm in Miss Pedler's and made a few feeble upping movements. Miss Pedler said: "Couldn't lift pussy, you couldn't." Apsley-Hunter burst into one of her frequent floods of tears and rushed out into the sluiceroom. That, I knew from experience, was the last I should see of her until the beds were done. I couldn't think why Sister and Staff Horrocks let her get away with it. If anyone else had thrown fits of temperament half as often she would have been out on her neck in as much time as it takes to shake down a thermometer.

When I ran into Pirie again, entering things in the temperature book on Sister's table, I said: "If it's taken him three months to get around to the sisters, it'll be January by the time Staff gets a look in. Then it'll take you in April and me in July." I reflected with some satisfaction that Apsley-Hunter would have to wait another fifteen months for her turn.

"In theory, yes," she agreed. "Only we shan't be here after this month."

I had quite forgotten to allow for that. The more I thought about leaving Ward 7, the more depressed I got, and there was nothing I could hum that fitted except *Autumn Leaves*, and that always made me want to cry, so I kept quiet.

By a quarter to eight we had more or less finished all our jobs, except the laundry; and Pirie pitched into Apsley-

Hunter, who was out in the bathroom dabbing her eyes with cold swabs, and told her to do that.

"Keep your fingers crossed," I told Pirie. "Three empty beds and no admission——" Then the telephone rang. I ought to have known I shouldn't tempt Fate.

It was Peter, in Casualty. He said: "I'm sending a woman straight along to you. She's very ill, and I'm tied up with a car crash as well."

I knew better than to have any personal chitchat with him at that juncture, so I said, "Right!" and went in to tell Staff Horrocks, and then organised hot bottles and shock blocks and the hypodermic tray, and put screens round the corner bed.

When the woman arrived on the Casualty trolley the porter gave me a look that meant: "This one looks dicey to me." I have been a nurse quite long enough to know that when a person looks dicey to a Casualty porter—or to an O.P. or theatre porter for that matter—then that person is certainly in a bad way. So I was glad when Staff Horrocks and Sam came shooting down the ward on parallel beams as soon as I had got her tucked up.

"No note with her?" Staff said.

I shook my head, and said knowledgeably, to impress Sam: "She's very dehydrated. Will you want a drip?"

Simultaneously Staff Horrocks said: "She's very collapsed. I'll get the drip things organised."

So Sam, knowing when to take advice, said: "We'll have a drip set up right away. She's in poor shape."

As soon as Staff had darted into the annexe I said: "Can you cope?"

He was muttering to himself, something about hypoglycaemia and pigmentation and shock, and while he pondered I looked at the admission slip. "Her name's Mrs. Andrews," I said helpfully. "If I were you I'd belt in some dextrose in saline. And I shouldn't think deoxycortone would come amiss either."

By the time Staff reappeared he had written up five per

cent dextrose in one and a half per cent saline, continuous drip, and was already scrubbing up ready to cut down for it. She said: "Well? What does he think it is?"

"An Addisonian crisis," I said promptly. "He'll want deoxycortone too, won't he?" I checked over the tray she had brought, set for cut-down.

When she shot off again, her eyebrows up in her hair—because although Dr. Cheshire is known to have a flair for endocrinology even if his practice is fairly general, we don't often see an Addison's at Thickers—I told Sam what I'd said.

"Why didn't I think of it first?" he said. "I'd have got there in the end, but I hadn't got that far yet. Look, if it *is* an Addison's I'd better not bung in anything but the drip until the boss gets here."

"Is he coming in?"

"I rang for him right away."

I blinked. "Look, you *can't* just go fetching consultants in like that. What will Mr. Franks say? And the R.M.O.?"

"They're both off call. . . . Come on, is the tray ready?"

Pirie brought the drip stand and tubing and paraphernalia and helped Sam to set it up while I kept an eye on Mrs. Andrews, who was mighty flat, and strapped the cannula in place on her ankle. I was just arranging a cradle over her cuddle-blanket when Dr. Cheshire came very quietly round the screens, leaving Staff to bob about over the top.

He looked over Mrs. Andrews very carefully, his eyes and fingertips alert, even though he was so quiet and gentle, and then he looked up at Sam. "Well?" He looked ready to take Sam's opinion seriously, which I thought was kind and generous of him, since his own was obviously already crystallised.

"Addison's in crisis, I'd say, sir?"

"Hm? On what evidence?"

"Well the—the characteristic pigmentation, sir, and the . . ." He reeled off his reasons. Meanwhile I noticed a trickle of stale blood at the corner of Mrs. Andrews's mouth, wiped it away and took the opportunity to look inside the mouth.

Dr. Cheshire was saying: "Yes. I wonder what sparked it off?"

I tapped my teeth with my fountain pen and looked hard at Sam.

"Could be tooth extractions, sir," he ventured.

Dr. Cheshire looked for himself. "Could be," he admitted. "Three within the last few hours. . . . Could be. Well—dextrose and saline, I think. That what you've set up?"

"Yes, sir. I wondered——"

"Leave it at that for the next few hours. We'll consider cortical extract when she's less collapsed. We'll have a blood sugar, too."

"Very good, sir." Sam made a note and looked intelligent.

"No letter from her G.P.?"

"No, sir," I said. "There was a bit of flap on in Casualty. Could be there's something there."

He looked at me for the first time. Because it was late in the evening the light over Mrs. Andrews's bed was glinting on the faint beginnings of a beard, like fine tinsel on his jaw, and his eyes were in pools of shadow. He said: "You've been studying tray-carrying technique, then? The steak Diane was better than horse, I trust?"

"Much better, sir," I agreed, before I really took in what he was saying. By the time I did he had stopped noticing me.

Then he nodded to Sam and said, "Nice work, Brown," and the two of them went up the ward side by side. After a while Sam came back. He looked mystified.

"Look," he said, "the Chief seems sure that this *is* an Addison's, but he says that I didn't have enough evidence to go on, and that I oughtn't to jump to conclusions. Now I've to do a whole list of tests, even though he says he's sure. . . . So how the blazes could *you* tell?"

"Oh, I couldn't," I said. "Not on the physical signs. Nor could he."

"Then how——"

"I told you her name was Andrews," I said. "She's been in here before. If I remembered her I'm darn sure *he* would."

"Then why didn't you say so?"

"There wasn't time, little one. And you didn't ask me."

Pirie whipped away the tray we'd used and said: "The night nurses have been here for ages. We'd better go, or there won't be any supper left that's fit to eat."

At the end of the ward, by the door, I could see Staff Horrocks's lace-edged cap bent over the report book in the bright light from the reading lamp. Our senior night nurse, a worried-looking girl named Goodwin who was scared silly of Staff Horrocks, was standing beside her listening intently, and I could hear the night pro in the kitchen rattling cups on to the trolley for the supper drinks. "Right," I said. "I suppose our busy little bee's still sulking in the sluice?"

"If you mean the fair girl with hair in her eyes," Sam mentioned, "she slid off about five minutes ago."

I sighed. "Nice work if you can get it." Then I checked that the drip was coming through nice and steadily and went into the kitchen to collect my cuffs and the lecture book I'd hoped to have time to revise from.

The night pro rolled her eyes up. "Have we got an ill patient?" What she meant was one who was very ill indeed.

"Fairly," I said. "An Addisonian crisis, if you've never seen one."

She was pretty junior, so it was more or less Greek to her. "Isn't it a sort of kidney thing?"

"Sort of," I said. "Anyhow, she's on a continuous drip, so keep your eyes open." I put my cuffs on and went to the table, waiting for Staff to notice me. Pirie seemed to have gone on ahead. After a while she looked up and frowned, then nodded unwillingly, so I knew that I could go.

There was nobody in the Bunny Run at all, because everyone else had gone on to the dining-room. But I didn't dare to break into a gallop, because at any moment Night Sister would come along on her preliminary prowl.

Sister Rhys-Williams has me on her black-list—where she has a good many other people—and I haven't a lot of time for her either. It's not that she doesn't know her job, but simply that—for me, anyway— she has a personality about as emollient as crude carbolic. She has a hardbitten, haggard face, opaque black eyes and restless hands, and in all the time I've been at Thickers I have never seen her smile. She is married, and lives out, which ought to be a humanising influence. Maybe it is. Maybe if she were single and lived in she would be even more like an irritable lizard, though that would be rather a tall order.

The reason she is so unpopular is because she has an unpleasant habit of saying poisonous things about practically everybody to practically everybody else, which naturally does not endear her even to those she leaves unscathed. Anyhow, if she caught me running she would have plenty to say, in addition to the remarks she frequently tossed off about my "vulgar laugh" and my "coarse voice". To be strictly accurate, I have a slightly husky voice, which is a family trait—Sam has it, too—in which it is impossible to coo. So has Sister Rhys-Williams, only hers has a kind of serrated edge.

Since I had no wish to hear it just then, I walked slowly and sedately along the Bunny Run, looking straight ahead, and I didn't know that Dr. Cheshire was following me until I turned right into the cloister dividing Ward 1 from the entrance block. Then he drew alongside and said: "May I borrow your scissors, Nurse?"

I whipped them out of the back of my belt and handed them to him, handles first. Then he used them, standing still at the corner, to take a neat V-shaped piece out of the centre of his left forefinger nail. It was the finger I had seen him fiddling with a day or two before. Now the edge of the nail was embedded in a painful-looking yellowish-white swelling. I said: "You've got a whitlow there, sir?"

"Yes, Nurse. I'm afraid I have." He handed me back the scissors. "I don't suppose that's going to do much good. I'm just going through the correct motions."

I looked at his fingers doubtfully, noticing that they had spatulate tips and waisted phalanges. Thoughtful and artistic, I thought. "That's all right for ingrowing toenails, sir," I mentioned. "I don't think it's going to help a whitlow very much."

"Then what would you suggest? A fomentation?"

I nodded. "Or mag. sulph. paste, sir."

"Perhaps you're right." He put his hand away in his pocket then and stood looking at me. "Nurse, I've been going to ask you——" He stopped because Sister Rhys-Williams was bearing down on us. "Good evening, Sister."

"Good evening, sir," she said hoarsely. She frowned at me. "Why are you hanging about here at this time, Nurse? You should be in the dining-room."

He held up his hand to quieten her. "My fault, Sister. I accosted Nurse Brown to borrow her scissors."

"Really, sir? There are plenty of scissors in the wards."

"I'm sure there are. Only . . ." He smiled sweetly, showing his slightly crooked front teeth. "Only I didn't want to walk back, you see."

She deliberately stood there, with her arms folded into her cape, waiting for me to go, so I couldn't do anything else. I said, "Good night, sir," and went on along the cloister to the front end of the Main Drag and crossed over to what the men call the Aviary, which is a kind of long curving conservatory, full of pot plants, which eventually leads into our dining-room over in the old building.

In the Aviary, which we use as a sort of auxiliary sitting-room in good weather, there are several wicker chairs and settees surrounded by palms and rubber plants. They make good sitting-out places when we have the monthly dances. These are usually held in the boardroom—an enormous panelled room which was once the ballroom of Thickbroom Hall. I caught myself wondering to which of these hideaways Dr. Cheshire would lead his partner at the October dance. My favourite place was an alcove surrounded by banks of shelving, holding pots of cineraria and fuchsia and smelling beautifully warm and greenhousey, where there was an old-fashioned wicker *chaise-longue* with two big wheels and handles for wheeling it out on to the lawn. Not that anyone ever did wheel it out: it simply stayed there, in the Aviary, and there was quite a bit of competition to hog it on dance nights, because it was in the quietest corner of all, away from the buildings. I had sat there many times with Peter Stead, and it was there that Val said goodbye to Jock Marston—or he said it to her—at the August dance. It seemed a most unsuitable place for Dr. Cheshire to take Sister Thorpe. Or Sister Mumby.

Val had kept me some supper, and a seat. "It's only scrambled egg with flaked haddock," she said, "but I thought you might be hungry."

She was in mufti, and I remembered that it was her evening off and that she was supposed to be out with Sam. I said: "I thought you were out on the razzle. How come you're in to supper?" I thought how nice she looked in her new lavender-blue suit.

"I'm supposed to be, but Sam had a hunch."

"What about?" I pushed away the unholy mixture and reached for the jam tart she had kept for me. "What kind of hunch?"

"Well, I met him at half-past seven, and when we got as far as the gate he said he had a hunch he'd better go back. And when we got back to the front office they were ringing round for him from Ward Seven."

I nodded. "That's right. We had a pretty bad admission."

"So I gather. And it was as well he *did* come back, because apparently he was on call, anyway. Mr. Franks and the R.M.O. were both out. You'd think he'd make sure, wouldn't you?"

"Bad luck," I said. "And you look so nice in that rig-out, too."

"Well, I'm seeing him after duty tomorrow, instead, when he really *is* off call."

"After duty?"

"Unless I can get someone to swop me an evening for a morning."

The odd thing was that Val ought to have been furious about having her evening spoiled, but she wasn't. She looked perfectly happy. "Aren't you wild?" I said.

She smiled, and it was one of those self-satisfied smiles. "No. I can wait."

She certainly had changed.

"As a matter of fact," she went on, "I've told him I'll see him in the Aviary, later on."

"But you *can't*!" It wasn't a bit like Val to go recklessly breaking rules. "The men aren't allowed there, unless it's a dance or something, you ass."

"Rubbish. I don't suppose there's really a rule about it."

"Well, I should think it's 'within the precincts of the Nurses' Home' for the purposes of the Act, as it were."

"Who on earth is to know? It's not lit, after supper. Home Sister never goes along there, and I don't imagine Matron has any reason to. Where else can I see him, if he's on call?"

"But if he's on call, how will they find him when they want him? Is there any coffee left?"

"Have mine—I don't want it. Well, there's one point in the Aviary where you can look across the garden through the Main Drag window and see the first light-indicator. He's red and white, and you can see that a mile off."

I knew just where she meant, too. It was the corner with the wheeled bed in it. It hadn't occurred to me that anyone else knew about the indicator's being visible from there. I had once looked over Peter's shoulder and seen his amber light pulsing in the distance. . . . "Oh, well. Don't say I didn't warn you."

"I won't," she promised.

After supper we all trooped into chapel. I tried not to catch Matron's eye, but there was nobody else in who could play the organ, and she tapped my shoulder as I passed her at the door. There is one thing about volunteering—if it can be called that—to play the organ; the privilege of choosing the hymn goes with it, except on special occasions. Most people choose something easy to play, so we get the Old Hundredth and Crimond a bit too often, and the really lovely tunes are neglected. I plumped for *And didst Thou love the race that loved not Thee?* but Matron said curtly, "No, Nurse. We sing that at Easter," and looked at me as though she thought it pretty C-stream of me not to know that. So I said very well then, could we have *All as God wills?* I think she thought I was being subtly impertinent, but in fact I wasn't. It's just a hymn I find comforting.

Whoever plays the organ has to wait until last to get out of chapel, and by the time I had been into the cubbyhole to switch the thing off Val had disappeared, so I simply sloped off to my room. I had a bath, and slipped on an ancient blue jersey dress, with the idea of going down to our common room for an hour to look at television by the fire. Then it all seemed too much trouble, so I leaned out on my windowsill sniffing in the damp smell of fallen leaves and chrysanthemums, and looking across the misty lawns to the flat stretch of ward blocks. Looking through the big lit picture windows of the Main Drag, between the departmental buildings, it was possible to get a pretty fair idea of what was going on in the hospital.

I saw Dan Chester, Mr. Lockyer's registrar, talking to Miss McGrail at the surgical end. Miss McGrail was the H.S. of the firm, so I supposed it was a legitimate conversation. All the same, it seemed to me to be going on rather a long time, and she was laughing a lot. I wondered how Peter would get on with her if he took over the registrarship from Dan, as he'd said he was hoping to do. Certainly she was in the right tradition, being dark, but she was rather the giggly kind, and that wasn't really Peter.

Down at the medical end I could see Dr. Cheshire again.

He seemed to be around rather late. I supposed they had taken in another emergency in Ward 7, otherwise there was no reason for him to be there at all. He was writing something on a slip of paper, using the wall as a desk, and the forefinger of his left hand stuck out stiffly as he steadied the paper. It must have been pretty painful. Then he moved, and I could see Smithson, the night pro from our male ward, standing waiting beside him. That meant that Sister Rhys-Williams must be there, too, because she would never have allowed a mere pro to chase him for anything. After a while they moved out of my line of vision.

I leaned there humming the evening hymn to myself. *All as God wills, Who wisely heeds to give or to withhold . . . And knoweth more of all my needs than all my prayers have told.* My needs were pretty complicated, I thought. It was good to think that maybe Somebody understood them better than I did. *I know not what the future hath of marvel or surprise* . . . I hummed. And then I saw Sister Rhys-Williams hovering by the window at the far end of the Aviary. She was saying something to Pritchard, who is Theatre Staff, and she looked pretty wild. She was emphasising what she was saying by thumping her hand against the windowsill, and twice she looked up towards the Home. Then I got it. There was a theatre case, and she had to call up one of the theatre people. At any moment she would go clicking along through the Aviary, slapping on lights as she went, because that was the quickest way through to the ground floor of our wing, where all the theatre people slept.

Without stopping to think, I tore down the stairs, along the bottom corridor, past the dining-room and the board-room and into the Aviary, which was still in darkness. I made for the alcove, going carefully so as not to send any pots crashing off the shelves. When I saw the red eyes of two cigarettes I said softly: "Val—are you there?"

"Lord," Sam whispered. "I thought you were a herd of elephants."

"*Cave*," I said. "I mean *cavete*. Sister's on her way. Go up through the boardroom corridor, you fatheads."

Val shot past me straight away, but Sam, who wasn't as familiar with the terrain, wasn't so quick. I was on his heels, pushing him in the right direction, when the lights came on and I heard the cross little tippity-tap of Sister Rhys-Williams's size fours.

We shoved Sam out at the side door, just past the boardroom, and went pelting upstairs to our rooms. Val said, "Thanks, pal," and then went off to have a bath. When Home Sister came up ten minutes later I was just unzipping myself and thinking about going to bed.

She tapped at Kerry's Luck's door, half-way along the corridor, and had a brief conversation. Then she came along to mine. I knew her footsteps well enough, but I said, "Oh, it's *you*, Sister!" when I opened the door.

She looked me up and down. "Nurse, have you been in the conservatory during the last quarter of an hour?"

It wasn't a crime; it wasn't forbidden. I said: "Yes, Sister. As a matter of fact I have."

"I see. With whom?"

That was a facer. I couldn't involve the others. And I hadn't strictly been *with* them. "Alone, Sister."

"Doing precisely what, Nurse?"

"Well . . . nothing, really, Sister. Just thinking. Humming to myself, and thinking."

It did sound feeble, and I wasn't surprised when she didn't believe me. But when she said, "Very well, Nurse. You can see Matron at morning office," I stared at her.

"See *Matron*, Sister?" It did seem a bit like using a mastoid hammer to crack a thermometer. "But why?"

She wheezed with annoyance. "I think you know why, perfectly well, Nurse," she told me. Then she closed the door and plodded away to the stairs.

I told Val when she came back from the bathroom. "Morning office," I grieved. "It's a bit steep. What did I *do*, for Pete's sake?"

"Did we knock anything over? Maybe Matron's pet begonia's got broken or something." She frowned. "D'you want me to own up too?"

There wasn't any point, I said. It was difficult enough to explain why one nurse was wandering about in the Aviary at night. To explain away two would be more than twice as difficult. Anyone could sulk alone, but two people brooding together wouldn't sound in the least convincing. And if we said we'd gone there to smoke Matron would launch into her favourite spiel about how she'd gone to endless trouble and expense to rig up the old gunroom as a nice little smoke-room for us, and now nobody used it.

Of course nobody used it. A quick drag in a bedroom, or in our common room, where it was taboo, was one thing. An officially permitted cigarette in an unheated little room furnished with six chairs, a coffee table and two large ashtrays, specifically for the purpose of being smoked in—such a horrid habit—was another. One was enjoyable, the other wasn't. Sin was pleasurable, in fact, and licensed debauchery was not. So nobody ever used the smoke-room. If we had gone in there we should have had about as much joy from our occasional cigarettes as licensed drug-addicts must get from shots administered on the National Health by the local G.P. Less, in fact. If Matron had only known it she could have turned us all into non-smokers in a fortnight by announcing that in future smoking would be permitted everywhere in the Home.

"There's no need," I told Val. "Lord knows what complications we'll be in for if you do. Leave it. By tomorrow morning I'll know what the score is, and then if it would help to split the responsibility I'll tell you. All right?"

People who were up for morning office had to go to first break, do without coffee in order to change into clean aprons and line up outside Matron's door at nine-thirty.

When I asked Sister Mumby if I might go she said: "Yes, Nurse. And I'm surprised at you. You've been quite a different person this week, but you've never done *this* kind of thing before." I noticed that her new hairdo was very elaborate, and I wondered where Dr. Cheshire would be taking her that evening.

"I don't really know quite what I've done, Sister," I said.

"Well, if you don't, who does, Nurse?"

Matron evidently did. When she condescended to stop signing things—which is a sort of unnerving device she uses when she wants us to feel cowed—she said: "I will not have this kind of behaviour, Nurse."

I looked at her silver inkstand and kept quiet, waiting for her to be more specific.

"You know perfectly well that you do not chatter to residents; you do not entertain *any* men friends within the Home precincts without special permission; you do not run away when a superior officer calls you."

"No, Matron," I agreed.

"Do you deny that you were in the conservatory last night—and *smoking*, too—with one of the residents?"

Sam's white coat, I thought. Night Sister must have seen it as I pushed him through the end door. And all she had seen of me was a flash of blue—which could as easily have been Val. It seemed hardly fair, when I considered that I had only gone down in order to warn her. At least, though, I didn't have to take the whole rap. "I wasn't smoking, Matron," I said with perfect truth. "Honestly."

"Then how is that there are cigarette-stubs with——" She hesitated, wrinkling her bony nose in distaste. "With *lipstick* on them, on the floor of the conservatory?"

"I don't know, Matron. They definitely weren't mine. I didn't have any lipstick on, actually. I'd just had a bath and——"

"Then did you see someone else there?"

To look mulish seemed the best answer to that.

"Very well. Then you'll kindly tell me the name of the man."

"The man, Matron?"

"Yes, Nurse. The man. Oh, we know he was there. I presume you weren't unaware of his name?"

That was one of those questions like: "Have you stopped beating your wife?" If I said I didn't know his name it sounded as though he'd been a pick-up in the dark; if I said I did she'd ask what it was. I said: "No, Matron."

"I see. You don't intend to tell me. I'm afraid your loyalty is a little misplaced: a man who would behave in such a furtive way and who would encourage a young nurse to disobey my rules is scarcely a person who can command any admiration." She paused and signed some more of the letters lying on her desk. I suppose she saves them up from the day before, because Camilla—a rather nice girl from the general office who also acts as her secretary—could never type so many between nine o'clock and half-past. Then she said: "I've been considering what to do with you, Nurse. I think that I shall have to move you away from Ward Seven and send you somewhere busier, where you'll have less time to chatter to the medical residents. You can report to Outpatients, straight away."

I was rather surprised at my own reaction. Normally I would have wanted to dance with delight. A female medical ward is nobody's idea of heaven. In fact, it's the last place anyone would actually choose to go, even though we know we have to have the experience and that it has to be somebody's turn to look after the poor women who also, presumably, don't choose to be there. Most people, asked to put their choice of work in order of preference, would say first Theatre, Casualty or O.P., then male surgical, female surgical, male medical and female medical. Matron—though I was sure she didn't realise it—was really doing me a favour by sending me to one of the top places in anyone's list. Yet I wasn't pleased. In fact, I was a little sad. I should not be sorry to see the back of Apsley-Hunter and Staff Horrocks, but I still didn't want to leave Ward 7. This in spite of the fact that Sister Branker, in O.P., was as easy to work for as a favourite aunt.

"Very good, Matron," I said.

"I shall tell Sister Branker that you are there to take surgical clinics and help with minor operations," she reminded me. She was evidently quite sure that whoever I'd been dallying with in the Aviary came from the medical side.

It wasn't until I was half-way down the Main Drag on my way to O.P. that I gave any thought at all to the fact that Casualty was next door to O.P., and that I should almost certainly be seeing a fair amount of Peter.

CHAPTER THREE

OUTPATIENTS is like any other departmental block at Thickers in that it is built on the uniform basic unit plan of two long wards end to end. The idea of all this uniformity is that any block can be converted to wards in an emergency by ripping down the partition walls. One can only imagine that in that case the departments like Physio, and O.P., and the dispensary, and the labs, and X-ray and so on, would all find themselves functioning in tents or maybe Nissen huts. Anyhow, since there's no Bunny Run bisecting the blocks on that side of the hospital, none of the departments except O.P. and Casualty are connected. Between these two there is a sort of entrance hall, leading off an ambulance park which is a tributary of the drive to the main gate. The outer part of each is made up of a waiting hall and registration office. The part nearest to the Main Drag is divided into consulting-rooms in O.P. and into cubicles and dressing-rooms in Casualty. Off the Casualty hall there is a minor ops theatre and small recovery ward. Both departments are Sister Branker's domain, but Staff Williams runs O.P. and Staff Timmins runs Casualty, each with her own team, and never the twain should meet if everything went like clockwork, which it rarely does.

Staff Williams, looking faintly surprised, bore down on me as soon as I went through to the waiting hall. "Yes, Nurse?"

"Matron sent me, Staff," I told her. "I'm supposed to be taking surgical O.P.s. Oh, and minor ops."

"I see. You'll be replacing Nurse Hobbs, I take it? She's been sent to Ward Seven."

I said I supposed I would. Hobbs, I guessed, would not be pleased.

"Have you done O.P.s before, Nurse?"

I'd done gynae, I said, and a short spell with Dr. Sweeney's allergies. And I was willing to learn.

The Alaskan Lullaby nodded expressionlessly. Not a single blue-black hair was out of place, and her dresses were four inches longer than anyone else's. She might have been the frontispiece for a life of Miss Nightingale. "All my O.P.s are covered until this afternoon, Nurse. Go across to minor ops and tell Staff Timmins she can borrow you this morning. Come back here at two, please." She glided away like a waxwork on invisible wheels. I was dismissed.

There was nobody in minor ops, nobody in Casualty hall except the two juniors, sorting out repeat dressings from fresh disasters, and nobody in the range of cubicles except one senior pro coping with six patients at once. I said: "Where's Staff Timmins?"

The senior pro, a girl from my own P.T.S. set, named Jackson, pushed back her wild cap and blinked at me. "Isn't she in the duty-room? She should be. Tea's up."

I had forgotten until then the rather pleasant privileges there are in O.P. and Casualty in the food and drink line. Nobody ever has time to go to coffee, or even to meals sometimes, at the statutory hours. So there is always a pot of tea on the go, and often sandwiches and buns from the canteen as well. I knocked at the duty-room door and found Staff Timmins—a small round bustling type—pouring out for

Peter Stead and Mr. Birch, the C.O. Mr. Birch ranks some-where between the registrars and the R.M.O. and R.S.O. and is the only senior man—except Dr. Weatherby, the Pathologist—who lives out. He is tall and pale, bald at the front and frizzy ginger at the back, with a long lugubrious face like Alastair Sim's and the sweetest nature in the world. Children adore him and so does everyone who works with him. He said, "Get out!" and grinned.

"Yes, Mr. Birch," I said, and went in. Peter smiled, and I smiled back cautiously.

Staff Timmins looked up when she had sugared their tea. "Have you come to help us?" I think she was quite pleased to see me.

"Yes, Staff. Actually I was sent to O.P., but they seem to be organised, so they shot me over to you. I've to go back at two."

"And when are you off?" She pushed a cup of tea at me.

"This afternoon. But I shan't be, now."

"In O.P.? Not likely. That's their busy time. It's all evenings down here, I'm afraid. Sister Branker's sure to give you one."

"Good," I said. "Evenings are quite my favourite passes."

"And if you don't get off till six-thirty you automatically get a late pass, now," she informed me. "New concession. And not before time, either. Whoever heard of getting off on time down here?"

"Goody gumdrops," Mr. Birch said. "You'll be able to kick over the traces, Nurse."

Peter looked at me queryingly. "Maybe Nurse has been sent down here as a penance for doing just that?"

"That's it," I agreed. "Entertaining men in the Aviary."

Staff Timmins laughed, dismissing the idea. "I'd like to see anyone try *that* on! What were you really doing?"

"I told you. Matron thinks I'm safer away from the medical side."

Peter looked sinister. "Ah, I see it all now. It's that new H.P."

"That's it. Not that Matron has any idea. She tried to get me to tell her his name. She simply didn't believe I was there all alone communing with the pelargoniums."

"You should have told her you were studying astronomy, my dear," Mr. Birch said. "It's a wonderful excuse for so many things that Matron doesn't quite understand." He put his cup down and went.

Staff Timmins looked at her notebook. "Minor ops, Mr. Stead. Nurse Grainger ought to have them lined up by now. Off you go. You can help in dressings, Nurse, until the thick of them are done. Then you can come into the theatre."

"Remind me," Peter said as he went. "We must take a look at Ursa Major sometime." He winked, holding up eight fingers, one doubled.

"Yes, Staff," I agreed. I was quite sure that Staff Timmins had no idea that an assignation had been made right under her nose. Nor did I know why I had made it, except that after being on Matron's carpet, and being uprooted from Ward 7, I felt I was entitled to a little compensation. Even if it was only to look at Ursa Major with Peter, and to pretend that he didn't run around with people like Lawson, which was understandable, and Staff Williams, which wasn't.

I went along and piled into dressings until there was only a single row left, which the junior could manage, and then went over to the minor ops theatre. Mr. Birch was opening a cervical abscess and Peter was anaesthetising. "Gown up," Staff Timmins said. "You can take over now, Nurse. I've had enough of these two."

So I found the gown drum and fished one out. In minor ops we don't have to be strictly aseptic, but we do start clean, and we do scrub up between cases. Mr. Birch said there were a couple of arm fractures waiting to be put up, and a face for sutures, and we'd do those next. Staff sent them in one at a time, and we coped with them. Then she brought us, the worst first, five men and a girl with pretty nasty glass cuts. Something had gone wrong with a bottling machine at the local pop factory.

The girl was very upset. She was a pretty little thing, with a heart-shaped face and silky yellow hair, and she had a three-inch cut slicing clean through her left eyebrow. She held Peter's hand and said: "I'll have an awful scar, won't I?"

He was very sweet to her. When he was talking to her as if she were his little sister I forgave him a good many things. And then when she was under, Mr. Birch put three clips across the cut to hold it while he put in neat fine sutures. When he took the clips out again I could see it was a beautiful job. "Right," he said. "Clean it up, Nurse, and let her have a good look in a mirror before we put the dressing on. Then she won't be taking it off when she gets home." He was very pleased with himself.

After the girl had gone Mr. Birch went off to look at a motorcyclist the ambulance had just brought in, and Staff went with him. Peter and I were left to clear up, which meant that I did it while he hindered. In the nicest possible way, of course.

He was hindering pretty fiercely while I was trying to scrub instruments at the sink, and I had just turned round and was standing at bay with a nice sharp rat-tooth forceps in my hand when the door bumped open and Dr. Cheshire, very pale, slumped down on the anaesthetist's stool and groaned. Then he put his head down on the table and passed clean out.

I swivelled the stool, stuck his head right down between his knees and held him there until he said, "Phew!" and sat up again. He still looked pretty unsavoury to me, and there were beads of sweat on his forehead.

Peter said, "Are you all right, sir?"—which seemed a fairly fatuous remark to me, and did absolutely nothing.

"It's his finger," I murmured. "He's got a pretty filthy whitlow. I expect he's banged it or something."

Peter came across then and took Dr. Cheshire's left hand

and pulled faces at it. It was now a purplish colour right up to the wrist, and the finger itself was tight and shiny, like a sausage about to pop. "Set for incision," he told me. I pointed out that so long as Dr. Cheshire had my hand in a vice-like grip with his good one I could do no such thing. He knew where the things were, I said, and he could get them himself. He got them. Then he fetched Mr. Birch away from his casualty so that one of them could fiddle with the gas apparatus.

Even when they rolled him on to the table Dr. Cheshire still hung on to my hand, and by the time they had opened his finger and drained it, and packed it, and given him a jolt of penicillin, I was beginning to think I should never be able to hold a fountain pen again. But quite suddenly he opened his eyes, let go my fingers and said: "Have I been a nuisance to you people?"

Mr. Birch beamed at him and said that he would have been a much greater nuisance by tomorrow, because we weren't really equipped for amputation in Casualty. "Blew up quickly, didn't it?" he said.

"Yesterday." Dr. Cheshire looked at me. "And Nurse was quite sure that mag. sulph. paste would do the trick. . . . Then this morning I caught the blasted thing in the doors of Ward Seven. I was very nearly sick all over Sister Mumby." It conjured up quite a picture. I thought then of Sister Mumby's new hairdo, and wondered whether he would be able to take her out, after all. I didn't see how he could possibly drive a car, or manage a knife and fork, or even make light conversation. Not, of course, that any of this was my business, but he seemed to me a rather solitary figure, and I had no idea who there was in the background to make these things easier for him.

At this point Staff Timmins came in to drive me off to lunch. "If you've to be in O.P. by two you'd better hurry," she said. "I'll clear up here—and thanks for your help."

It had been a pleasure, I said. I took off my gown, found

my cuffs and went. Peter waved with one finger, but the other two men didn't see me go.

I had hoped to see Val or Hobbs at lunch, but I was much too late. There were only a few theatre girls still in the dining-room, and a little huddle of people from Physio and X-ray. We didn't mix much with the physiotherapists and radiographers. They had a table of their own where—or so it seemed to us—they carried on high-pitched and joyless conversations on subjects totally outside the range of hospital gossip. They lived out, of course, and they excited themselves about council elections and protest meetings, and a great many other things which seemed to us a little un-real. They tended to be spectators of the hospital scene in many ways, and at fire practices they often made a great play of protecting their expensive equipment without bothering to rescue the patients first, which struck us as faintly amusing. They did mingle once, when our favourite princess came to open the new X-ray department, and stood in the drive uttering staccato little cheers of the kind heard at the end of a women's hockey international, but by and large we had little in common. All of which is the reason I found myself reduced to talking to Coralie Lawson while I hurried through my lunch.

She said straight away: "How goes the Thorpe–Mumby contest?"

I said that I didn't know there was one, and that in any case I was now seconded to O.P.

"Oh? I heard you were up for office. What have you been up to?"

"According to Matron," I said, just to intrigue her—and she is very easily intrigued—"I've been caught snogging in the Aviary."

"And weren't you?"

"In fact, no." This she clearly thought was pure fabrica-tion. "But Sister Rhys-Williams says I was, and who am I to argue?"

"The Aviary? I never thought of that," she said. I could

see her pigeonholing the idea for future use. She looked at me with fresh interest. "Is it true you've been out with the new H.P.?"

"Yes. But he's very dull," I told her. "I wouldn't waste your time if I were you."

"No? He *looks* all right."

If I didn't put her off, I could see Val was going to have trouble on her hands. I knew that look. It was difficult. If I said Sam was fast it would make him more interesting to her; if I deplored his slowness she would see herself as having a mission to teach him a thing or two. "The trouble is that he—he *sniffs*," I said. "All the time." Then I thought of something else, even more calculated to deter her. "And he's terribly mean. He borrowed a fiver from Peter Stead— goodness knows if Peter will ever see it back. My dear, he tried to borrow from *me*!"

"Then you weren't with *him* in the Aviary? So who was it?"

"I wasn't with anyone."

"You mean—you weren't with a houseman at all?"

"Right."

"You surely weren't with a *consultant*?"

It was very silly of me, but because Dr. Cheshire was the only consultant I was really on speaking terms with, and because the very idea of being alone with him, in the Aviary or anywhere else, was practically *lèse-majesté*, I felt myself blushing. "How absurd can you be?" I said. "I'd better go, or I'll have Staff Williams giving me fifty lines or something. She *is* a bit schoolmarmish, isn't she?"

"That," said Lawson, off on a new tack, "is not precisely what *I've* heard. She speaks of marriage."

I stopped in my tracks and held on to a chair. "Of *what*?"

"Marriage," Lawson said. "Mr. Right has come along at last and she means to have him. Her mind is made up."

"I don't believe you."

Lawson shrugged. "If it's true he won't stand a chance. She's a very determined type." That, coming whence it did, was probably accurate. It takes one determined woman to recognise another.

"Poor Peter," I said. "I wonder if he knows?"

"*Peter?*" Her eyebrows went up. "Who said anything about *Peter?*"

"I heard they've been out together."

Lawson burst out laughing, which was unusual for her. "He gave her a lift to the station on her day off," she said. "And she insisted on giving him half a crown for the petrol. Big deal."

That was something of a relief. It also rang true.

Sister Branker lolloped across to me, pushing back stray bits of her loose corn-coloured hair, and said breathlessly: "Oh, Nurse. So nice to have you. Take Mr. Lockyer, will you? Don't forget, *all* new patients to him, specials to Mr. Chester and routine checks to Miss McGrail. All right?"

"Yes, Sister."

"That's right, Nurse. Eric has begun on the cards for you." She pointed across to the filing cabinets outside Mr. Lockyer's rooms, where the O.P. porter, too short to reach otherwise, was standing on the bottom drawer to get at the top one.

I went over to him. "All right, Eric. I'll do the As and Bs."

"Oh, it's you, Nurse Brown, is it?" He climbed down again, grinning. "I told Sister to keep me a tall one."

"Did you, now? Well you've got one." I looked along the little row of waiting patients in our section. "Many more in the big hall?"

"I haven't looked yet, Nurse. I reckon to bring 'em through in sixes, see. There can't be many yet. But this appointment system's not working, I'll tell you that. Three for two-fifteen, three for two-twenty-five, three for every ten minutes. And the whole lot still come trooping in at two. So you may as well take them as they come, like we used to. First come, first served. They *like* waiting. It's an afternoon out, and a chance of a gossip, if you ask me."

"I'll go and check," I said. I went through to the big hall and found five more waiting in the right place, and another six among other people's patients. The only way to herd them together was to stand on a chair, clap my hands sharply and call out: "Anyone to see Mr. Lockyer?" After I'd done this twice I managed to sort them out from the crowd. I made a list of their names and took it back to Eric. He could go on finding their O.P. cards while I checked the rooms.

The outer room of the two was a large one with desks at each end for the registrar and the H.S., and four examination cubicles. Beyond this was Mr. Lockyer's own room, which had a desk and a single couch in it. Staff Williams had already put out the junk on the desks. They all had the same tray, spatulas, sphyg, hammer and so on, but Mr. Lockyer had his own auriscope and ophthalmoscope set, whereas the other two had to share one. The racks were already stocked up with the various bits of stationery— X-ray forms, path. forms, physiotherapy requests and the rest—and there were clean blotters all round. If I'd been on duty there during the morning all that would have been my job. It was a relief to find it done for me.

Miss McGrail came down first. I said: "Will you have the checks in now? I've got three ready for you."

"I don't usually begin till Mr. Chester comes," she said. "I mean, I might want to refer to him." In other words, she didn't altogether trust her own judgement, which was better than not admitting it, I felt. "But if there are any due for discharge . . ."

I knew how she felt. "There's one you could get rid of," I suggested. "An old fracture. Physio recommend discharge now." I fetched the man in from the front row and sent him into a cubicle, and then Dan Chester arrived.

"Where's Nurse Hobbs?" he wanted to know.

I said she'd been moved.

"I don't know," he grumbled. "As fast as I train 'em they take 'em away. And as soon as I get you into line they'll do it again. I can't keep a nurse in this clinic for more than three weeks." He looked up and grinned. "All right. Roll 'em in."

"What about the N.P.s?"

"They'll just have to wait till His Nibs comes. He shouldn't be long."

In fact, Mr. Lockyer was nearly twenty minutes late. By then I had the traffic flowing smoothly in the first room and seven new patients waiting outside.

He is a smallish man with a red face and red scrubbed hands, and he has a breezy manner which makes him seem lacking in concentration. In fact, he is an extremely good surgeon, and since he has small hands and is neat-fingered, he has a reputation for making the smallest incisions in the hospital. He can get away with an appendicectomy scar about half the length of anyone else's, and his cases, being less shocked than most, always seem to do well. He is really a general surgeon, but a lot of G.P.s look on him as being the prince of the peritoneal boys, so most of his referred cases prove to be abdominal. It was therefore a little unusual to find that his first new patient was a woman of about thirty with a large bluish naevus on her cheek which she wanted removed.

"I think we'll see what carbon dioxide slush will do for that," he decided. "Fix her an appointment, will you, Nurse? Of course it may not respond, and in any case it will take a little time, Miss Hinks."

"I was hoping you could just—well, remove it," she said.

"Surgically? Not if it can be done otherwise. We don't want to leave unnecessary scars, do we?" He didn't add that it might be dangerous.

"But I'm—I'm getting married in six weeks' time."

"My dear girl . . ." Mr. Lockyer spread his hands. "Does that make so much difference? Your fiancé won't——"

"You don't understand." She looked across at me. "He's —he's never *seen* me."

Mr. Lockyer frowned. "Never *seen* you?" Then he began to laugh. "I'm afraid I don't understand."

"I do, sir," I said quickly. I could see she would burst into tears if she had to explain. "You mean this is a pen-friend engagement? He's abroad?"

"That's right, Nurse. In the Falkland Islands." She blew her nose. "He's had a lot of photographs, of course, but they only showed the good side. And I couldn't somehow tell him. I thought——"

"Bless my soul!" Mr. Lockyer said. "Aren't you taking a bit of a risk? Well, never mind, let me look at that naevus again." I passed him the ophthalmoscope battery with a magnifier attached, and he went over it again. "All right," he said at last. "We'll see what we can do. Nurse. . . . Fix a bed, will you? And I'd like Dr. Weatherby to see this, too. Will you make an appointment for us to fore-gather?"

"Yes, sir. I'll ring his secretary as soon as I can."

"Good. Good. Right, Miss Hinks. We'll do what we can. But no promises, remember!" He opened the door for her himself.

As he closed it his face changed, and he shook his head. I said: "No good, sir?" I was thinking of his possible reasons for calling in the Pathologist.

"What a dreadful business," he said. "Poor girl. We must get a biopsy, of course, but——"

"You mean it's become malignant, sir?"

"I'm pretty sure. Poor girl! And what a fantastic way of carrying on a courtship!"

"Yes, sir," I said. "But maybe she hasn't had a chance of any other kind. You'd be surprised how men shy away from anything in the least odd."

"And women don't?"

"Oh, no, sir. Actually a man with a scar is usually con-sidered to have extra fascination!"

"You don't say so? Good gracious me! How very odd. Well, next time I cut myself shaving I shall console myself with that thought. . . . And now the next patient, if you please, Nurse."

I brought in the next—a man with a cervical cyst—and went out to ring Dr. Weatherby's secretary, and to arrange for Miss Hinks to be admitted, and in the hall I ran into Sam. "You and your love-life," I said. "Look where you've landed me now!"

"All right," he said. "I'll go and own up. Relax."

"It wouldn't help, you fathead."

"Then what can I do to soothe the savage breast?"

"Nothing," I said. "Yes. Yes, there is just one thing."

He salaamed. "Hearing is obeying."

"Is it? Well, I'm giving you the gipsy's warning. Lawson has her eye on you. I've told her you sniff, and that you're mean, and that you borrow money from girls. So just you play it that way."

"You're so helpful," he said. "Remind me to do the same for you sometime. Next time I see a fresh chap breathing heavily in your direction I'll repay the favour. I'll tell him you like garlic, and that your teeth aren't your own." As he went on down the hall he looked back over his shoulder and grinned. "I'll tell him you snore, too," he said loudly. Very loudly.

It is at moments like this that friends of Sam's hope to remain unobserved. I did not. Staff Williams appeared at my elbow and said frigidly: "Nurse Brown, please! Remember that in Outpatients you are representing your profession to the outside world. You are making a very unfortunate impression."

It would have been so easy to explain, to say: "Oh, he's my brother, Staff. You know what brothers are." But out of sheer perversity I didn't. And it wasn't until I'd done my telephoning and given Miss Hinks her date that it occurred to me to wonder who Staff Williams's newly arrived Mr. Right was supposed to be. I couldn't imagine having *her* as a sister-in-law. And she was just the kind to be bowled over by Sam's boyish charm, as people called it, because she was so inhibited herself. I had seen it happen before. The most unlikely women took to Sam.

When I got back to my clinic Miss McGrail had things in a fine tangle. There were five people for X-ray, all hanging about because she still hadn't signed the forms, and she had referred three more across to Dan Chester before he was ready for them. So the room was packed and everyone was complaining. It took some time to get things organised again before I could go back to Mr. Lockyer, and when I did he sent me to find him a cup of tea. There would be some going in the duty-room, I knew, so I walked straight in. Staff Williams was in there alone, and she was crying. Drinking tea and crying into it, instead of being at her desk out in the hall. This was so shaking that I couldn't say anything. I simply walked out again, and got the tea from the canteen instead, and in the canteen I ran into Hobbs. I told her, of course.

She said: "It must be something Lawson said to her, then."

"*Lawson?*" I wasn't with it at all, I told her. "Why Lawson?"

"Because she's just been into O.P. to take some pensioned-off theatre gloves. I saw her. And when she came out she had the look in her eye of having just dropped a little poison. You know."

I knew all right. And I had a nasty feeling, for no reason at all, that I was involved. Or that Sam was.

I didn't see Staff Williams again until after half-past six, because it took me until then to clear up the clinic, take the specimens across and put all the O.P. cards back in their files. When I'd finished at last I took my O.P. gown off and found my cuffs and went to report off. She wouldn't even answer me when I said: "May I go now, Staff?" She turned her head away from me and nodded, and that was all. For once I stuck my neck out. I said: "Is there anything wrong, Staff? Anything I can do?" I really felt sorry for her because she looked so bleak.

"No, Nurse Brown. There's nothing *you* can do," she said, in a choked sort of voice.

I wondered why the stress was on the "you", but I said that in that case I'd better go.

"Yes," she agreed. "I think you'd better." Disaster, her voice implied, was imminent if I didn't.

It was all very mystifying.

I met Peter in the car park at half-past seven. He was sitting in his car smoking a cigarette while he waited. When he saw me he climbed out. "Can you still drive this crate?" he said.

"I think so." After all, he had taught me. "Why?"

"Well, I've promised to deliver the Big Cheese's chariot. He went home by taxi. I thought you could follow in mine and pick me up. O.K.?"

"O.K.," I agreed. "Where does he live?"

"In some flats, at Hill . . . something or other Court. Where the farm used to be, you know."

I knew. I had been furious when that particular block went up and obliterated the last bit of green in its neighbourhood. But I'd heard that the view from the top was superb. "I know," I said. "You go on, and I'll follow."

He lost me after the first hundred yards, of course. The big grey saloon was out of sight before we reached the first island. And when I got to the flats at the top of the rise neither Peter nor the car were there. He must have taken it round to the garage, I decided. The best thing I could do would be to wait until he turned up. Two cigarettes later he was still missing, so I got out and walked across to the entrance hall. Dr. J. J. M. Cheshire, I noted, had the top flat on the right. If Peter was still up there gossiping it was high time he was reminded that I was waiting, I felt. The lift was there, on the ground floor, and I walked into it and pressed the top button.

Once on the quiet top landing I wasn't so sure. I stood outside the white door reading the typed label—*Dr. J. J. M.*

Cheshire—and wondered what all the initials stood for. As far as I was aware, nobody had yet found out. *James James Morrison Morrison Wetherby George Dupree*, I thought. Could it be James? Or John? Jeremy, perhaps. None of them suited him very well. He needed something more masculine. . . . Then I heard Peter's laugh inside, and rang the bell.

Dr. Cheshire came to the door himself. He stared at me, and then his smile came out like the sun, just for a second. "Good evening, Nurse."

"Good evening, sir," I said. "I wasn't sure whether Mr. Stead was——"

A cloud came over the sun. "Oh, I see. You're looking for Mr. Stead." He stood aside. "Do come in, won't you."

Peter got up from the armchair by the fire. "Lord," he said. "I forgot you'd be waiting. Sorry, Brownie." He looked across at Dr. Cheshire. "She followed with my car, you see."

"He should have told you to come straight up, Nurse. You'll have a drink now you're here? Sherry?" He was faintly smiling as he poured it. "There. Now do sit down."

I always do as consultants tell me. Then I looked at his bandaged hand. "Are you more comfortable, sir?"

"Much, thank you. Thanks to you and——" The telephone rang.

He sat with his back to me on the arm of the deep settee while he answered it. But after saying: "Yes . . . She *what*? But that's absurd!" he stood up and moved away, frowning. "No, of course not," he said. "What?" He was looking at me now, and his face was buttoned up tightly with annoyance. All the opal tints left his eyes. "Oh, she did? . . . You're sure? Now look, my dear, you're making—— *No*. No, I've said so . . . No . . . Well, I'll talk to you tomorrow. Goodbye." He put the receiver down very carefully and stood looking at the carpet for a moment. Then he said: "Well, thanks, Stead. I expect you want to be off now." He walked to the door without giving me time to finish my drink. And as he let us out he neither spoke to me nor looked at me. I felt terrible.

Back in Peter's car I said: "What on earth was all that in aid of?"

"All what?"

"Why, practically throwing us out headlong! I hadn't even drunk my sherry."

"I'll buy you another."

"I don't *want* another! I only had that one to be matey, you ass. What was he so wild about, all of a sudden?"

"Maybe his girl friend stood him up."

"He stood her up, tonight. Poor old Sister Mumby, she had a new hairdo and everything. . . . I hope he remembered to put her off."

"He did. Or at least he rang somebody from Casualty and said he couldn't make it. . . . Yes, it *was* the Mumby, because he said, 'Is that Nurse Horrocks?' when they answered."

"I wonder who rang him tonight. It was a woman, anyhow."

Peter sighed. "Look, you are out with me, love, or are you more interested in the Big Cheese?"

"I'm out with you," I said. "*And* I've got a late pass."

Peter squeezed my right knee.

When we got back to the car park, a good deal later, Sam's car was still out. I said: "Let's wait till Val comes in. She shouldn't be long now."

"All right, let's." Peter put his arm round me again. "Coming to the October dance with me?"

"Who, *me*? What about Nurse Lawson? And Staff Williams? And all your other friends. You don't want to——"

He kissed me, hard. "Quiet! I don't know why you have to persist in seeing me as little-friend-of-all-the-world. I'm not. But I don't go around wearing my heart on my sleeve, because it wouldn't make life any easier for either of us, in a place like this."

"That's what you tell all the girls, I'll bet," I said.

"If you're going to be like that . . ."

"Yes?"

I suppose I asked for that one. It went on a long time, and when he let me go I wanted to cry because it was so much like old times. "That's more like it," Peter said.

"Like what?" I pushed him away and began to tidy my hair.

"Like my girl."

I sighed. "Peter, I'm *not* your girl. And you're about as much mine as—as the Co-op is one member's."

"You keep saying that. And it isn't true. What *do* I have to do to show you?"

I was not going into all that again. "You'd have to dance every single dance with me at the October dance," I said lightly. "Goodness, that would shake them!"

"You know I can't do that. I've at least eight duty dances. Haven't we all? You couldn't turn down the R.M.O., for example. I couldn't not ask Sister Branker. And so on. We do have to *live* in this place."

Just then Sam and Val drove in, with exactly a minute to spare. I said, "Thanks for a nice astronomy lesson, Peter," and got out.

Val said: "What astronomy?"

"Galaxies," I told her. "Peter's an expert on them."

We left the two of them in the car park and trotted up to our rooms. Val, I thought, looked extremely happy. I only hoped she would be allowed to stay that way. She said: "You're not weakening, are you?"

"About what?"

She looked in my mirror and smiled at herself, pushing her hair into place. "Peter, of course."

"I don't know why you say that. You know darned well how I feel about Peter. You ought to, by now."

"Quite." She turned round again. "That's what I mean. So why pretend you don't?"

I sat down on the bed and took my shoes off, keeping one in my hand to wave at her. "All right. I like Peter. Peter is attractive, and clever, and a pretty good doctor. What's more, he excites me. There are times when he makes me feel that my bones are turning to cherry brandy. And when I watch him being sweet to kids, or people who are scared, I'm not really responsible for what I feel. But that's all. *All*." I threw my shoe at her, and she caught it neatly.

"But what more do you want?"

It was very difficult to explain. "I want someone more— more self-contained. Someone who's a person to himself and doesn't need other people's reactions to make him tick. Peter . . . Peter simply adapts himself to whoever he's with. He's a sort of . . . multi-adjustable all-purpose Romeo when he's with a girl. On his own he isn't a complete person at all."

"I wouldn't say that. The other men like him."

"But I want a man other men *respect*. It's different."

"You know what?" Val looked at me pityingly. "You're greedy. You're not satisfied to have a man you can be happy with. You want to be able to put him on a pedestal, too. You can't have it both ways, old dear. No man is perfect."

"No, I suppose not. And if I did find one who was . . . he wouldn't look at me. It's stalemate, then. I'll do my State Final, then my midder, then a year or two staffing and doing sister. Then Admin. . . . Then I'll be a Matron and buy a little dog to keep me company because there won't be another single soul in the entire hospital that I'll be able to be myself with."

Val didn't sympathise at all. She went to bed. But before she went she said: "I'll diagnose. You're in love, and you won't admit it." That just showed how besotted she was with Sam. Her judgement had gone completely overboard. Nobody was more detached, just then, than I was. I caught myself humming my old favourite again as I undressed.

Whatever the future might have of marvel or surprise, I was very tired.

From seven-thirty to nine in the morning the work in O.P. consisted of laying out the clinics ready for the morning sessions. Staff Williams, like Sister, didn't come on until nine, because of working late. So it was Middleman, the senior pro, who gave me my job. "It doesn't matter who does what," she explained, "so long as it gets done. Well, you've been here once before, so you know. But I do like to lay out the clinics I'm going to take, so bags I Orthoptics. I'll do Dr. Berger's O.P. too. Then you can lay for Dr. Sweeney —you've done allergies, haven't you?—and Mr. Holtby."

"Which do I take?"

"Dr. Berger or Dr. Sweeney. Staff does Mr. Holtby herself, and there's no more surgical this morning. She'll tell you, when she comes."

Mr. Holtby's rooms were exactly the same as Mr. Lockyer's, and took no time to lay up. Dr. Sweeney's allergy clinic was a lot more complicated. As well as all the ordinary diagnostic things, there were racks of testing phials, and more racks of desensitisation media, and a whole battery of syringes, scarifiers and so forth. Whoever had done the clinic the week before had not re-ordered several of the testing bottles: we were out of half a dozen of the various pollens, dog-hair and horse-hair, and they were all important. I had to go along to the dispensary straight away for replacements, and by the time I had waited for old Mr. Dixon, the boss-man, to put on his white coat and organise himself for the day I was a quarter of an hour behind.

Sister Branker flopped in at Dr. Sweeney's door and sat on the edge of the table to look round. "Oh, yes. Very nice, Nurse. Are all your bottles full?"

"They are now, Sister. Some of them were out."

"Oh. Good. Well, you'd better take Dr. Sweeney, then. There'll be the H.P. to help you."

"Mr. Cork?"

"No, we've a new young man. That's what I came to tell you. Mr. James. So you'll have to show him the ropes, won't you?" She got up and leaned on the doorpost. "I don't know what we shall do with you this afternoon, I'm sure. I can't put you on Special clinic if you've not done it before, and Staff Williams always—— No. No, it's her afternoon. She asked for one specially. . . ." She wandered off without coming to any useful conclusion. She would, I knew, finish her thinking aloud as she went through the waiting hall. It helped her to clarify her thoughts, I suppose.

Dr. Sweeney and his new H.P. arrived together. Whoever worked with Dr. Sweeney would also act as H.P. to Dr. Belman, the heart man in Ward 1, since Dr. Sweeney was purely an O.P. consultant and had no bed allocation. If any of his allergies were ill enough to come in as in-patients he had to borrow beds where he could. I looked up from the desk as they came in. When Sister had said, "Mr. James" it hadn't conveyed very much. But now I saw that in fact it was Simon James, no longer a serious fifth-year but a qualified houseman.

I said, "Good morning, sir," to Dr. Sweeney, and smiled at Simon.

Dr. Sweeney, tall, grey and very quiet, said: "Ah, you again, Nurse Brown. You know Mr. James?"

"We have met, sir. When he was clerking."

"Good. Well, you put him wise, will you? Many waiting?"

"Fifteen, sir, so far. You want the new ones yourself, I expect?"

"Yes, please. Mr. James will stay with me for a time, if you'll carry on with the routine injections, just to get the picture. . . . Come along, young man."

I led the patients through to them one at a time, and brought in batches from the hall for their weekly desensitising injections. I had done most of them when Simon came through, and there was time to talk. I said: "Long time no see, Simon."

He looked just the same. Square, brown, good-tempered. Very keen on his job. He said: "I was lucky, wasn't I? Somebody let them down, or I'd have had to wait. How are things with you?"

"Much the same, I think."

"Still semi-detached?"

"I wouldn't say that. Quite detached, really."

"Really? Then could we have dinner sometime?"

"That would be lovely, Simon," I said. "We'll talk about it. Right now I've some check-tests for you. All right?"

"Just a minute. . . . I look at the ones who didn't react, see if there's a late flare-up, and if so I give them another shot?"

"Right. You also see people who've been partially desensitised and have fresh symptoms. And if we get people with exacerbations of symptoms who don't react to any darn thing, then you refer them for psychiatry. O.K.?"

"O.K. Wheel them in, then."

I went in to Dr. Sweeney to see that he had enough clean needles and reagents. He called me over to the girl he was testing. "Look at that."

There were about forty different pricks on the girl's arm. No real reaction from any of them. "Yes, sir?" I said.

"Something wrong with the mixed pollen, I think. See this top one? That's it. Not the faintest reaction. But I'll bet she reacts to rye-grass. . . . There . . ."

Together we watched the fresh patch come up, red with a white centre.

"You want Mr. Dixon to check the batch, sir?"

He shook his head, and passed me the girl's card. *Referred to Dr. Vincent*, I read. I raised my eyebrows. Dr. Vincent was our visiting psychiatrist.

Dr. Sweeney was saying: "So I want you to see a colleague of mine, before we go ahead with treatment. Just to check over your general problems."

The girl frowned. She was thin and dark with grey shadows under her eyes. "What problems, doctor?"

"My dear, we all have problems. And they can affect our health."

"You mean—you don't mean this is *mental* trouble?"

He smiled encouragingly. "No, no, no. But I think you're tired and worried and you need a little general help. If you wait outside Nurse will make you an appointment." He got up and shook hands as she left. Not many consultants did that, and I like to see it. Dr. Cheshire, I noticed, was always sure to touch the bed-patients when he saw them, if it was only to make a show of checking their pulses. The patients felt that they had gained something from him, I was sure.

When the girl had gone out of the room Dr. Sweeney said: "Now you're puzzled, hm?"

"Yes, sir, a little."

"Well, I'd sized her up as the suggestible kind. I'd already done a rye-grass spot with no reaction. Yet when I suggested to her that she would react to it she obediently did. She doesn't have asthma, or hay-fever, or urticaria, whatever she thinks. She has an outsize conflict."

"I wonder what, sir."

"I know. She doesn't realise how much she told me. She's thirty. She wants to get married. Her young man says it's now or never, because he's offered a job overseas. Her mother won't be left. So she retreats into asthma every time there's an argument about it. That way she effectively puts off any decision."

"But sir, even if she's—even if this is explained to her, and she accepts it, she still won't be any nearer deciding."

"No? Look, if she gets to the point of realising that any decision is better than none she'll decide. And if it's the wrong decision her symptoms will continue. Then she'll know, won't she?"

I suddenly felt very strongly about this. No doubt Dr. Sweeney, who didn't profess to be a psychiatrist, could be wrong. All the same, it wasn't my business to say so. But I said so nevertheless.

"I just *don't* agree, sir," I said. "Look, I'm a girl. I could be in that position. I'm not, because my parents are globe-trotters and they don't need me like that, but I can imagine how it would be. And I'd like to bet that if that girl sees Dr. Vincent her asthma will get worse. Because, having more insight, she'll feel even guiltier whatever decision she makes."

Dr. Sweeney wasn't angry at all. He listened. And then he said: "All right. I'll have a small bet with you. Half a crown?"

"All right, sir." I put mine on the table, and he did the same.

"Mr. James had better hold the stakes, I think! How is he doing?"

"All right so far, sir."

"Good. Any more for me?"

"Only one, sir. I'll bring her in."

I took the next patient in, and then fixed the girl's appointment with Dr. Vincent and gave her a reminder card. She said: "I reckon I get this asthma thinking about all that snow in Canada. I can't stand the cold. But I'll have to go, because if I don't do it now I never shall."

"Whereabouts in Canada?"

"British Columbia," she said. "Not far from Vancouver, I think."

I laughed. "If you see snow there I'll be surprised. It's a perfectly wonderful climate. My father travels all over the world, buying timber and so on, and he says British Columbia is the nicest place he goes to."

From the expression on the girl's face it didn't seem to me that she was going to need Dr. Vincent at all.

I waited until Dr. Sweeney and Simon had finished, and I was collecting up the cards for filing, before I said anything. Then I held my hand out to Dr. Sweeney. "Five shillings, please, sir."

His eyebrows twitched. "Oh? Has she decided already?"

"Yes, sir. You didn't let her talk long enough. She thought Canada was entirely composed of snow . . . hence the asthma. Or so she says."

"Ah, so she *says*. Patients *do* try to rationalise, Nurse. No. Mr. James will continue to hold the stakes until we see what Dr. Vincent says, I think."

He went on ahead of Simon, and Simon snatched a moment to say: "Are you free tonight, Brownie?"

"Yes," I admitted. "Yes, I am."

"Eight o'clock?"

"All right, Simon. Thank you."

When Middleman came through to close the windows and lock up she said I looked as if I'd gone into a trance. I said: "No, I was just thinking. I sometimes surprise myself."

Staff Williams, waiting to depart for her afternoon off, was in charge when I left for lunch. She said: "Nurse, I have something to say to you."

I went on pulling my sleeves down. "Yes, Staff?"

"I think you'll have to be very careful indeed to see that you speak the truth. Otherwise you are going to find yourself in very serious trouble."

I stared at her. "Speak the *truth*, Staff?" Now what was wrong? Had she discovered that Sam and I had been doing a little leg-pulling?

"Yes, Nurse. You—you have tried to involve a man of integrity—and importance—in a very nasty situation." Her pale face reddened and her hands were trembling. "I consider you owe Dr. Cheshire an apology. It is only his generosity that prevents him from going to Matron about it."

I felt as cold as if I had been slammed straight into an ice-pack. What colour I can have been I can't imagine, but I felt grey. When I managed to breathe again I said: "Dr. Cheshire . . . I simply don't know *what* you're talking about, Staff! What is it I'm supposed to have done? Or said?" I waited, but she didn't say anything. "If you won't tell me, Staff, I shall have to ask *him*."

She looked at me with infinite distaste. "Do exactly as you wish, Nurse. But I can assure you it will probably make the situation much worse. I imagine you want to finish your training?"

When I got to my room I wasn't cold any more. I was hot, blazing. The more so because there was nobody around I could tell. Lunch was something I couldn't possibly face. And somehow I had to calm down in time to begin on the afternoon O.P.s at two o'clock. Ever since Peter and I had left the flat I had been telling myself that I had imagined the sudden change of atmosphere. Now I knew I hadn't. Something I had *said*, Staff Williams had hinted. Something that wasn't true. Something that involved Dr. Cheshire. It was no use: I couldn't even think straight.

I washed my face, changed my cap and went back along the Main Drag to O.P.

CHAPTER FOUR

SISTER BRANKER was at the desk in the waiting hall, and Eric was already fishing out O.P. cards. I went over to Sister, taking my cuffs off.

"I shall have to do the Special clinic myself," she said. "Before you do it I shall have to put you in the picture . . . They like to feel that they're being dealt with by trained staff, you see. People of discretion. . . . Can you take over here until Nurse Middleman's free? Then I'm afraid you'll have to do Dr. Cheshire's O.P."

Afraid, I thought. Afraid? If anyone was afraid I was. I said bluntly: "Would you rather I didn't, Sister?"

"No, Nurse. But—— Well, Matron *did* send you here to do surgical. Nurse, you'll be good, won't you? *Don't* distract the H.P., dear."

"Distract the—— Me? Sister, of *course* not."

"Well, there have been complaints, Nurse. . . . Not from me, don't think that. So do be good." She looked over at the side door where Specials came in and went straight into their clinics without waiting in the hall. "I'll have to go. Nurse Middleman won't be long."

Eric came across to me and murmured that he'd got out all the cards for Dr. Cheshire so far, and he would keep an eye on the new arrivals for me.

"Bless you," I said. "He's not here yet, is he?"

"No. Nor Mr. Franks, nor the H.P. I'll give you the wire when they come."

Actually I arrived in the outer room a moment after Dr. Cheshire had gone into his. I didn't go in to him at all. If he wanted me, I thought, he would buzz. And as long as he didn't buzz I would merely keep the flow of traffic going steadily in. Mr. Franks and Sam had their hands full with their own quota, and all I needed to do was to test specimens and deal with appointments for special reports. I kept up with the two of them somehow, and saw that as one patient left Dr. Cheshire there was another ready to go in.

Then the buzzer sounded. I needn't have worried. After one look Dr. Cheshire turned away from me. "I'd like a specimen here, Nurse. Test for sugar, please." He smiled pleasantly enough at the man who was sitting on the couch putting his shirt on. "Go with Nurse, will you, Mr. Bolton? I'll see you again afterwards." Then he looked at my belt as though he had never seen me before, and said: "Next patient, please, Nurse. And shouldn't you be chaperoning?"

"I'll come back when I've tested, sir," I promised. It wasn't the time to explain that I'd thought he'd prefer me to keep out of his way.

After that I went in with every patient, waited until they were undressed, escaped when they did. When Mr. Franks had a batch of tests waiting I did them all in one go while Dr. Cheshire was examining a man who would obviously take some time. I didn't talk to Sam at all, and I had an idea that he'd been warned, too, about idle chitchat. He was certainly a good deal quieter than usual. But then, he scarcely had time to be anything else.

I had gone to the hall to chase up a woman who had gone

off without her X-ray chit when the men went, leaving the place in chaos. It took me half an hour to tidy the outer room, and then a fair time to file the cards. It must have been nearly six o'clock when I got around to sorting out Dr. Cheshire's room. It was something of a shock to find him still there. The usual procedure was for his team to see him off at the front door after he'd had tea in the consultants' room. This thought made me say, although he was busy writing notes: "I'm sorry, sir. There wasn't time to fetch you a cup of tea. Would you like one now?"

He looked up absently. "No. No thank you. I shall be off in a few minutes." His finger still stuck out stiffly from his left hand, and I wondered who was driving him. "Please tidy in here if you want to."

It was by no means the thing to tidy round a consultant, but I got on with it, sorting the cards, putting away the ophthalmoscope and other things he had used, straightening the couch and taking off the used pillowslip. When there was nothing left to do I fastened the window and turned off all the lights except the anglepoise on the desk.

He slapped down the last card and said: "Sit down, Nurse."

One of the things nurses may never do in the presence of a superior officer is to sit down, which means that only ward sisters ever have an opportunity to rest their legs, and they need it least. And even a ward sister would not be seen dead sitting down with a consultant within a hundred yards, except in the canteen. For me to do so was plain unheard-of. So I didn't. I simply stood there.

"Please," he said. "Sit down." Because he was either impatient or nervous all his Australian accent came out on that "down". He made the request sound like: "Siddayun." He meant it, all right. So I sat down that time.

"Now look," he began. "I don't know whether you're crazy or whether you're just young, but by God, don't you try to make a monkey out of me." He chewed his bottom lip for a bit. "I thought you were a nice girl. Maybe you are

I don't know. But don't you ever again put me in the position of having to deny a lot of stupid women's tittle-tattle about you and me, or we're going to quarrel. But quarrel. . . . I hate having to say all this, but it was screaming to be said. Well, I've said it." He stood up then, looking very tired, and went over to the window, looking out into the dusk with his back to me. "Now," he said, "will you be so good as to dress this finger for me, because it's extremely uncomfortable."

I fetched the things without speaking, for the very valid reason that I couldn't. And by the time I was putting fresh gauze on his finger—which was still discharging, and looked rather more than sore—he looked up at my face and said: "I've no objection to a saline dressing, but it isn't what was prescribed." And then he used his good hand to reach up and mop my face for me with his clean handkerchief. He didn't smile, but he didn't look angry, either. His changeable eyes were dark blue with a kind of sorrow. Rather like a father who has to thrash his son, and at the same time knows that the son's sins are his fault. A guilty sorrow, in a way.

When I'd fetched the thimble and tidied off his dressing I said: "Sir—this is two lectures I've had today, and I still don't know what either of them have been about. I think you'd better explain. . . . If I've done anything to annoy you, or hurt you, I'm sorry. Only I don't know what it *is*."

"I almost believe you," he said. "I *want* to believe you. But I think my sources are pretty reliable."

"Would you care to—to quote your sources, sir?"

"I'd like to very much. But I gave my word."

"That was hardly fair, was it? I get no opportunity to answer the charge if I don't know what it is."

He looked down at the desk, frowning. "Well, I'll put it to you. But it's embarrassing for me as well as for you. . . . Have you said anything at all, to anyone here, to indicate that there's been—that there's been anything between you and me?" His cheekbones were touched with painful colour. My own face, I knew, was flaming. "Well?"

I had no idea who had said what, or why. I only knew I hadn't. And quite suddenly—surprising me more than him, probably—I completely lost my temper. "It's odd," I said. "A moment ago you were a consultant physician and I was a half-trained nurse. . . ."

"And now?"

"Now, suddenly, it's not like that. I don't have to call you 'sir'. I don't have to look up to you. You're a man, and I'm a girl. You're a lot older than I am—fourteen or fifteen years older. And I don't know how you dare insult me by asking such a question. I think you must be conceited, and brutal and uncivilised, to be able to talk to me this way." I took a deep breath. "And now I'll tell *you* something. I hear tittle-tattle, too. And some of it sounds true. There's one bit that's just fallen into place in my mind. Maybe you'd like to know that Staff Nurse Williams is talking about the wonderful man—'Mr. Right' is the phrase that's been used—who's just entered her life. She plans to marry him, whether he likes it or not. . . . And to judge from her frenzied defence of *you* this afternoon it's pretty clear who she means."

I walked out and left him sitting there. If I'd gone to report off I should very likely have hit Staff Williams, so I simply walked out of the department, up the Main Drag and across to the Home. And then I lay on my bed and cried till my face was sore.

At eight o'clock, feeling as though I had just surfaced after too much nitrous oxide, I went slowly along to the main gate to meet Simon James. I didn't want to go out, I didn't want masculine company; all I wanted was to crawl into a small hole and quietly die. But Simon was a nice boy: there was no reason to hurt his feelings as well as my own. What was perhaps even more important to me just then was that he, and any distance he might put between me and Thickers, would be an escape for an hour or two.

He was waiting in the layby in a prim little black saloon,

old but shiny, and he got out and handed me in, in his usual polite way. "I do hope you won't be bored," he said, "but I remembered I'd promised to go to a concert, and I thought you might enjoy it too. If not, we won't go."

Now the very word "concert" instantly raises all kinds of doubts in my mind. At school we were dragged off to concerts willy nilly, and most of them were quite dreadful, because I am allergic to all kinds of fiddle-scraping and modern scales with no semitones in them. I am also allergic to sopranos with too much vibrato and basses like muffled dinner-gongs. My taste is all for rich noise, like Beethoven and Tchaikovsky, and I like singing to be about something —unless of course it is a boy's voice, in which case almost anything goes. So I said cautiously: "What *sort* of concert, Simon?" I crossed my fingers against Bach and Handel.

"Oh, a rather jolly one. All Gilbert and Sullivan stuff. Now that the ban's off, anyone can have a crack, you know. It's at Sutton Town Hall and it doesn't begin till half-past. All right?"

I relaxed then. "Thanks, Simon. That will be lovely. I feel a bit dreary, so it'll take me out of myself, as they say." I sat back, feeling a good deal better, as he carefully turned the car. When we were on the straight again I said: "Who's doing this thing?"

"Ah, well, that's rather the point. It's being put on by B.U.D.S. and the Medical School. It's going round all the suburbs in turn, in aid of W.H.O. This is the first bash, actually. If it goes down well it ought to get good publicity."

"And why aren't you in it, then? I seem to remember you did rather well in the last show they put on." Simon had a light pleasant tenor voice, I recalled, which had gone down very well in some Schubert ballads.

"No time for rehearsals," he confessed. "I've been odd-jobbing in the theatres at Queen's for the last two months. Just for the hell of it."

I thought of something, then. "Did you run into Jock Marston, there? Used to be H.P. on Ward Seven at Thickers."

"Marston? Oh, yes. That's the chap who got married."

"*Married?*" He could have knocked me down with a diet slip. "Jock's married? When?"

"Last month. No, six weeks ago."

That meant very soon after he'd left Thickers. "Simon, who did he marry?"

"A girl from——" He turned his head to look at me briefly. "But of course, you'll probably know her! She's working in Physio at Thickers now. Gerry Hollins. Well, I suppose she's called Gerry Marston now."

"So *that's* why . . ." I told Simon then about Jock's departure in mid-stint. But I didn't say anything about Val at all. "We all wondered why he went like that," I added.

The conversation fell through then because we had arrived and Simon managed to park the car outside the old fire station. The square was packed.

"Looks like a full house," I said. "I suppose this is a good district to open in, though. Everybody around here is mad keen on amateur theatre and opera, and all that." There were a lot of people milling about in the foyer.

"That's what we thought," Simon said. "This way, I think. We've got seats in the fifth row."

I was glad we were near the front, because I knew from experience that the acoustics are rather odd in the Town Hall. There's a kind of dead patch in the middle of the floor where things can be almost inaudible which are clear at the back. When we were settled I looked round to see whether I knew anyone. After a minute or two I nudged Simon and nodded along the row in front. "Matron," I murmured. "*And* the R.M.O." Not that Matron looked at all authoritative without her cap. In fact, she looked rather like any other elderly woman, and she was wearing some tatty-looking beads round her neck which merely emphasised its scragginess. Not at all the sort of person anyone would be scared of. It just showed what a difference uniform could make. I supposed that Hitler, in a sweater and old slacks, would have got nowhere fast; whereas in the

T.V. oldies I'd seen of him it only took a swastika or two, and a too-big military cap, to reduce arm-waving crowds to gibbering hysteria.

"Lots of Matrons, in fact," Simon pointed out. "Look." There were five more, very much like ours, all in a row at the front. And next to them a real glamour-puss. No chicken, but beautiful. Simon was looking at her. "She's from Queen's," he informed me.

"What is she?" Only Night Sisters ever look like that. Sister Rhys-Williams is utterly atypical.

"Matron. I told you."

I stared. A neat and lovely hairdo, a clever face and superb eyes. "I don't believe it. No Matron *could* look like that."

"Well, she does. She thinks nurses ought to look as pretty as possible, for the patients' benefit, and she believes in setting an example."

"She must look smashing in uniform."

"She does. None of your starched caps, either. Just a little frilly affair—a bit like a white chrysanthemum. Popped on top like a wedding hat, you know."

I could imagine. I was still comparing her with our specimen when the lights went down and the orchestra began the *Pinafore* overture.

If I had made out the programme myself it couldn't possibly have contained any more of my favourite scraps in the time. We went from *Pinafore* to *The Mikado*, from the *Yeomen* to *The Gondoliers* and back, via the *Pirates, Ruddigore* and the rest. A ballad here, a chorus there, and the audience trying not to join in, as I was. Simon pointed out several people I knew or had heard of among the singers, and when little Mr. Lockyer stepped forward to sing the Duke of Plaza Toro, and the Major-General, it was an unexpected joy. I looked round to see whether there was anyone else from Thickers to hear him, but I could see only Matron and the R.M.O., both looking faintly deprecating. I don't know why, because he was Lytton to the life—if my old discs are anything to go by—and he carried it off beautifully.

We stayed in our seats during the ten-minute interval, largely because Matron and the R.M.O. went out and there wasn't much future in bumping into them in the bar. I couldn't imagine Matron drinking anything more aban-doned than tomato-juice, but out she pushed all the same. Simon didn't mind a bit. "It's a frightful squash out there, anyway," he said. "Hardly worth the battle."

I settled down for the second half happily enough. There were at least another eight items to come. Unfortunately I only really heard two of them properly. When Frederic trooped on with Mabel and the *Pirates* Chorus, I registered only that he was—as they usually are—tall and fair, and rather thin. And then he began to sing. I listened, entranced.

> *"Who would not give up willingly*
> *All matrimonial ambition,*
> *To rescue such a one as I*
> *From his unfortunate position . . ."*

He had a glorious voice. Idiotically I gripped Simon's hand. "It *is* him, isn't it?" I said. "Isn't it?" Simon, I think, was a little embarrassed. He nodded silently. I sat forward on the edge of my seat, concentrating myself into my ears.

> *"To such a one, if such there be,*
> *I swear by heaven's arch above you . . .*
> *If you will cast your eyes on me*
> *However plain you be I'll love you . . ."*

He made the most of the cadenza at the end. And while his Mabel got on with *Poor Wand'ring One*, leaning on his chest, I was still hearing him.

"Nice voice, Cheshire," Simon murmured in my ear as he gave me my hand back. "He's been professionally trained, you can tell. Of course, all Aussies are great ones for singing, aren't they? Like the Welsh."

"Are they?" I blinked at him, still dazed. "I didn't know. . . . I had no *idea* he could sing like that."

After that I took in very little until he came back for his duet with a girl named Jane Stokes, who, Simon said, was a fourth-year and a friend of his. I don't think I heard her at all, except that when she began:

"Ah leave me not to pine, alone and desolate;
No fate seemed fair as mine, no happiness so great . . ."

I knew I had only to wait a few moments for his:

"Ah, must I leave thee here, in darkest night to dream?"

"Relax," Simon said. "It's only a *song*."

I shook my head, because if I had spoken I think I should have cried. I went on listening to the golden voice:

"Where nature, day by day, will sing in altered tone
This weary roundelay:
He loves thee, he is gone . . ."

lingering on that high sad note, as it had on: *"He loves thee, he is here . . ."* And I wished with all my heart that I could have been a fourth-year named Jane Stokes and leaned there, in the curve of his arm, singing heartbrokenly with him.

Simon jerked me to my feet as they played "The Queen", and led me into the dark square when we had shuffled out, tight in the crush. "And I thought you were too flippant to react to 'the potency'," he said.

"Noel Coward wasn't talking about Gilbert and Sullivan," I protested. "He said *'cheap* music'. Anyway, I didn't. It was just that he has such a—a moving sort of voice."

"But I brought you out to cheer you up. And now you're all tearful."

"Not really." I followed him to the car, by the old Fire Station. "I'm not sad. Just sentimental."

When we were in the car, and turning out of the square into Anchorage Road, he said: "Not sentimental about Dr. Cheshire, I trust? Because he isn't the kind."

I flushed, thinking of my last conversation with Dr. Cheshire. "No. Definitely not," I assured him. "He's—he's hardly the type girls dream about, I imagine."

Simon dropped me back at Thickers a few minutes later, and I think he was a little fed up with me. Not that he said so—Simon is much too polite. He kissed my cheek politely and said: "Thanks for coming, Brownie. At least you weren't bored."

"No. No, I certainly wasn't bored," I agreed. "It was sweet of you, Simon."

He didn't ask to see me again, and I didn't blame him.

Val was drying her hair in the utility room. Even mob-capped by the green plastic hood she was pretty, I thought. Above the noise of the drier she said: "Nice evening?"

I nodded, and mouthed that it had been heavenly.

When she had switched off and uncovered her ears she took out the cotton-wool and eyed me curiously. "It can't have been Simon."

"What can't?" I began to roll up the flex for her. "You're not going to comb it out now, are you?"

"No. . . . It can't have been Simon who made you look like that." She filled the kettle and plugged it in, and I watched her get down the cups and saucers before I answered.

"Can't it? . . . Like what, anyway?"

She swung round to look at me again. "You look—you look the way I feel about Sam. And I don't believe you feel that way about Simon. In fact, I know jolly well you don't. So . . . ?"

"Oh, it was the music," I stalled. Not because I didn't want to tell Val, but because I didn't want to believe that there was anything to tell her. "I suppose I got a bit carried away. Gilbert and Sullivan does that to me."

"You didn't look like that when we went to the D'Oyley Carte session, old dear." She swung herself on to the scrubbed counter we use for ironing. "Come on, give."

"I wish you'd seen Mr. Lockyer," I said. "Just like a penguin, in his tails. And there was Matron, in a——"

"I said *give*." Val was laughing at me. "I don't imagine either of those two being the thrill of the evening."

Until then I had always looked on "thrill" as being rather a cheap little word. A little like "kick", only more old-fashioned. But when Val said it I knew it was the only single word there was to sum up what I'd felt. What I was still feeling. It was something I didn't want to think about just then, so I said: "Do you know a Physio type called Gerry Hollins?" That wasn't a very clever move, but it was all I could think of at the time.

Fortunately Val didn't rise. "No, I don't. And what has *she* to do with it? Don't tell me you've begun a beautiful new friendship!"

"No." I sat down on the ironing stool, defeated. "No, that isn't what I've begun." I suppose I was beginning to realise that I *had* begun something.

"Well, who else was there? We've disposed of Simon, Mr. Lockyer, Matron and somebody called Gerry Hollins. Take it from there."

I told her, then. Not what I'd felt, but just what I'd seen and heard.

She nodded knowingly. "Remember? I told you you were in love and didn't know it."

"How absurd can you be? With *him*? Look, he's been an absolute pig to me today. I've never been so humiliated in my whole life. Never. And I shall never forgive him. I shouldn't think he'll ever speak to me again, the way I lost my temper with him." I told her all about that, too. "The two things just don't hang together."

She made the tea and handed me a cup. "We'd better take this to bed, or we shall have Sister on our tails again. . . . The two things don't hang together, don't they? But they *do*. Don't you see, you simply aren't capable of being indifferent to him, are you? You have to react violently one way or the other. Lord, we did enough psychology in our first year for you to be able to grasp that."

"I detest him," I burst out. "I *won't* be stirred by him. The things he said . . ." And then I added illogically, "Besides, he's a consultant."

Val laughed so much that I thought all her pink foam rollers would fall out along the corridor, like an auguste's string of plastic sausages.

I lay awake for a long time that night, my mind shuttling between the two incompatible images. Dr. Cheshire, his face dark with anger, snapping, "Siddayun!" and, "Don't you try to make a monkey out of me." And then Frederic and Fairfax, and the tender clarity of the voice lingering on: *"He loves thee, he is gone . . ."* The two simply didn't mix —and yet they were inseparable. It was only when I tried to find analogies, and caught myself admitting that the most repulsive sluiceroom chores were equally inseparable from the drama of the theatre, and characters like Sister Rhys-Williams from those like Sister Branker, that I was able to relax and sleep.

I felt very guilty about Staff Williams next morning. So guilty that I might have gone to her and confessed exactly what I'd said about her if I had seen her when she came on duty. It was perhaps as well that long before she arrived there was a panic call from Casualty and all of us from O.P. shot across to lend a hand.

It was one of those things we all hate—a school bus, packed with children, had skidded into a lorry, and we happened to be the nearest hospital. There was no time to get them along to the Children's where they belonged, and seven ambulance loads were in our laps. Maybe if they had screamed or cried it wouldn't have seemed quite so horrible. The fact that even those with tear-stained faces were so controlled and quiet made it all much worse. Crying and hysteria would have been easier to face than all those wide, shocked eyes. And three of them, the ambulance men said, had died on the way in. We had two in each cubicle to begin with, and a lengthening row of stretchers in the hall, as well as a bench full of those who were shaken but apparently unhurt, all of whom would have to be examined before we could let them go.

Mr. Birch and Peter were fetched from their breakfast and began at once on the crush injuries and the worst lacerations in Minor Ops, using both tables at once. Jackson and Middleman and I and the others began clearing the rest as quickly as we could. When Staff Timmins came on she had Sister Branker with her, rolling up her sleeves as she bounced in, and they both joined us in the cubicles.

It was one of those times when there's a kind of glow in the work. Not because we were doing something that was urgent and valuable, nor because it was good to see the children getting over their fear as we made them more comfortable, but because we were all so busy and absorbed that there were no longer any barriers of rank or seniority between us. From Sister Branker down to the junior pro we were working together, as equals, not caring who did what so long as the job got done. More than once I saw Sister trudging back from the steriliser, and carting dressing drums about, and once she came across to me and held a little boy on her lap so that I could suture his cut leg. There was no time to wait for the men to do the simple stitching jobs, and normally Sister would have taken them over, but she said, "Carry on, Nurse," and didn't criticise when I made a mess of the first knot. That was how it went, right through. We were all equals together. It was a pretty wonderful feeling.

The glow carried over, after all the little ones had gone, when Jackson and I set to to deal with the backlog of regulars waiting for dressings. And at lunchtime, when we stopped working for the first time since eight o'clock, I was refreshed in a way I hadn't known was possible, in spite of my aching back and heavy feet. As I put on my cuffs to go to the dining-room Mr. Birch said: "Well, all that was very jolly, wasn't it?"

"Jolly?" I said. "All those poor little kids . . ."

"That's what I mean. We've all *done* something this morning. Very satisfying. You've enjoyed it, so why not admit it?"

I did admit it. "It's nice to feel useful," I agreed. "Especially after women's medical."

"Yes. I'm afraid the physicians have all the fun on the medical side. The pleasures of medicine are largely intellectual."

"I know," I said. "You don't even get a kick out of really nursing a pneumonia these days. Science has made it so much easier. There's no room for dedicated brow-moppers any more, it seems to me."

He smiled benevolently. "There is, dear child. There is. Good nurses are still the best medicine. All the same, you've been really *stretched* this morning. We all have. And just once in a way it's rather nice."

Certainly O.P. seemed very flat and quiet afterwards, even though the hall was full and there were four clinics going at once. I found myself sorting out new patients' cards for Dr. Belman's session with Simon at my elbow. He said: "Well? Recovered, have you?"

I smiled at him. "I suppose so. But it was mighty while it lasted."

"Mighty?" His neat eyebrows went up. "Strong words."

"Well, it was. All working in a team, you know, and——"

He said quietly: "I meant, had you recovered from last night." Fortunately he saw Dr. Belman's car, through the window, at that point and I wasn't called on to produce a sensible reply. And by the time he came back, trotting behind Dr. Belman and Miss Cooke, his registrar, like an amiable Corgi, I had the first five patients inside and three of them ready for examination, and there was no time for that kind of chitchat. It was just as well, because I could still not have been very coherent about the things that were going on in the dark little pigeonhole where I do my private thinking.

Dr. Belman, who is a large, comfortable, baggy man with a fatherly attitude towards nurses, hardly needed me. He said: "All right, Nurse. I'll buzz if I want anything. I expect you've got plenty to do." So I left him with the first new patient and went back to the outer room.

If Dr. Belman tries to make life easy for us his registrar certainly cancels out his efforts. Miss Cooke, tall and clumsy, with the kind of pale-blue eyes that always look completely expressionless, is just about as demanding as it's possible for a resident to be. She wanted specimens tested for practically every patient, X-ray, path. lab. and physiotherapy forms filled in ready for signing, and me hovering at her elbow at every second. Some of these things she got, when I wasn't busy seeing patients in and out and rescuing their cards before they made off with them. It was quite a time before I got over to Simon's desk, and when I did Dr. Belman buzzed for me.

He had a man in there, I remembered, who had been referred by his G.P. with a letter explaining that his original heart condition had now become complicated by occasional attacks which merited a second opinion. I went straight in. "Yes, sir?"

"Ah Nurse. Mr. Gurden here isn't in fact a new patient. He did attend here some years ago." He smiled at me, looking up over his glasses.

"I'm sorry, sir," I apologised. "The registration office had him down as a N.P., and——"

"Oh, I'm not reproaching you, Nurse. I'm glad I did see him. Now look——" He showed me the notes. "Partial heart-block, that was the original trouble, you see. Now he's having attacks of blackout and giddiness. . . . Would you take him along to Miss Pitter and get an E.C.G. done? He'd better rest for a bit, first. Then we shall probably find there's a ventricular asystole, I think."

I nodded. "Stokes-Adams attacks, you mean, sir?"

"Exactly. It sounds a classical case. The usual brief syncope, followed by vivid flushing and quick recovery. Still, he doesn't appear to have reached the fibrillating stage yet, so there's no immediate danger, as long as he takes things easily."

"I'll take him along in a wheelchair, shall I, sir?"

"Yes, I should. Not that he'll approve." Dr. Belman twinkled at me. "I'll tell him for you."

He went back into the examination cubicle while I fetched the chair and blanket. Miss Cooke called out: "Oh, Nurse! Where *have* you been? I want——"

"In a moment, Miss Cooke," I promised. "I've got a patient for E.C.G. first."

"What, *now*? Really, it's too bad!" She looked helplessly at the array of forms in the rack in front of her. "*I* haven't time to fill these things in." All the same, she was scribbling away competently enough when I passed her with the chair a moment later.

She was quite right, of course. It wasn't usual to interrupt O.P.s to get electrocardiographs done, but if that was what Dr. Belman wanted it was not for me to make difficulties.

Mr. Gurden, even in a wheelchair, was very breathless when I got him to Miss Pitter's room, so—as Miss Pitter wasn't there, and I would have to find her—I suggested he lay on the couch while he waited. Immediately I had him there I regretted it. Because he promptly passed out, and I couldn't feel his pulse at all. I stood there, holding his wrist, waiting for the beat to begin again and for the characteristic flush to replace his bluish pallor. Only the beat didn't return, and the flush didn't rise. There wasn't a thing that I personally could do, except to get a doctor, and fast. I ran.

I suppose I had intended to get Miss Cooke or Simon, but they were half the Main Drag away. When I cannoned into Dr. Cheshire and Mr. Franks I gasped: "Quickly—a collapsed patient. E.C.G. room." As they hurried back beside me I said: "Stokes-Adams, I think, but he hasn't come out of it."

Dr. Cheshire gave Mr. Gurden a brief look and said:

"Nurse, adrenalin, quickly. Half a mil., *long* needle." Then Mr. Franks put his clean handkerchief over Mr. Gurden's open mouth and began mouth-to-mouth resuscitation.

I had to get the syringe from Ward 1, because it was the nearest place, and I was glad that Staff Hall was on and didn't waste time asking whys and wherefores the way Sister Bragg would have done. When I shot back into the E.C.G. room with it Dr. Cheshire snatched it from me, looked at the needle, and drove it vertically into Mr. Gurden's chest. "Into the right ventricle," he explained. "That ought to do the trick."

Mr. Franks looked doubtfully over his glasses. "It's to be hoped he hasn't been having fibrillation," he said gloomily. "Might be dangerous if he has."

I didn't see how anything could be more dangerous than death, but I said: "No, he hasn't, Mr. Franks. Dr. Belman said so."

We all watched, then, as Mr. Gurden virtually returned to life. It was a little like a miracle, I thought. In a few minutes he was breathing normally and opened his eyes in astonishment to see the two men bending over him. "Have I had another turn?" he said.

Dr. Cheshire nodded. "You have. All right, now? Nurse will stay with you. You just relax." Then he turned to me. He smiled for the first time, and I knew that he wasn't smiling at me at all, but only to himself because he was full of relief and had to let down the tension somehow. "I'll see Dr. Belman and explain," he promised. "I suppose you're taking his O.P.s, are you?"

"Yes, sir."

"All right. Stay with him, and I'll fix things. He should be all right now." He checked Mr. Gurden's chest again with his stethoscope and then they both went out. And at the door he looked back and sent me another smile. This time it was for me. It completely wiped out all the things he had said to me the day before, so that when Staff Williams came to relieve me a few minutes later I even felt friendly towards her.

When I managed to escape from Miss Cooke again I went back to Dr. Belman between patients. I didn't have to tell him anything. He said: "Good for you, Nurse. Dr. Cheshire told me how quick you were. I've had that man admitted to Ward One. Thank you very much."

I hadn't done anything that merited any thanks, but it was pleasant to be on the right side for once.

Peter called in to see me while I was clearing up after the clinic was over. He grinned. "Hallo, Trouble."

"Now why that?" I wanted to know. "I'm as harmless as——"

"As a sucking dove. I know. But wherever you go there's something." He ran a forefinger down my back as I bent over the cards and got them in order for filing. "Had a collapse this afternoon, I hear."

"Oh? Who told you?"

"I heard the Big Cheese singing your praises to Staff Williams. Presence of mind, and all that jazz."

"What rot," I said. "I simply panicked and grabbed the first man I saw."

"Quite. There *are* those among us who wouldn't have been quite so quick about it, I gather. Anyhow, you're in good books again."

"Again?" I was unwise enough to turn to face him. He was still kissing me when the door opened and closed again behind me. "You idiot," I said. "Now my name's mud again. If that was Staff Williams——" I pushed him away.

"It wasn't," he soothed me. "She's gone to tea. Look— what *about* the dance? Yes? Or no? Speak now or for ever hold whatever it is. . . . I shall take someone else," he threatened, "if you don't say 'yes'."

I slapped the cards together tidily. "Who, for example?"

"Well . . . there's a nice little girl just started in Ward Six. Red hair. And there's your friend Ringway. Or there's the Apsley-Hunter job," he teased.

"You can't take Val—she'll be going with Sam, and I *won't* have you busting that up. I don't see you taking dear

Robina. But the red-head in Ward Six is a sweet little thing, straight from convent school and hardly up to your weight. So for her protection alone I'll accept . . . I think."

"You're slipping, love. The red-head—whose name, by the way, is Teresa O'Donnell, and may the divil look past her—has already been out with Mr. Holtby's registrar *and* houseman. Which is why, I gather, she was transferred somewhat hurriedly from Ward Ten to Ward Six. So save your protective impulse. Just come with me because you know you want to."

"All right. You know you're the only man I can really dance with. . . . I wish I was a foot shorter; I'd have more choice then!" I frowned. "Peter, are you *sure*?"

"About what, love?"

"About O'Donnell. Has she *truly* been out with Mr. Andrews, and with Pat Lyall?"

"So I'm told. Why? Surprised?"

"Very," I admitted. "For one thing Mr. Andrews is married. And Pat Lyall's supposed to be engaged, isn't he?"

"On paper, yes. But Andrews hasn't seen his wife for years. She went off with somebody else when he was C.H.S. And as for Pat's engagement, it seems to have worn rather thin."

"It will do," I pointed out, "if he takes out little girls of eighteen."

Peter smiled. "It was practically threadbare before she arrived. Not his fault, either. Seems his ladylove has her eye on someone with a little more spending-money."

"Then why doesn't he break it off? Taking other girls out isn't going to help, is it?"

"I have an idea that he thought that might work the oracle. He thinks breaking off engagements is a lady's privilege. He's simply been giving her a good excuse."

"It still isn't the right way to do it."

"No, love. But we are not Brother Lyall's keepers, are we? Nor Nurse O'Donnell's. Anyhow, I was merely making the point that she's not quite as unschooled as you seem to think. . . . And you can't go round protecting everybody, so don't try. Just come to the dance and protect *me*, hm?"

"All right," I agreed. "Now will you let me file these cards?"

"I'll consider it."

I pushed him aside and went out to the filing cabinet. Over in the duty room Nurse Middleman was fixing the dressing on Dr. Cheshire's finger. I knew then who had opened and closed the door of Dr. Belman's clinic room.

The canteen was nearly empty. I could see Sam down at the far end talking to Miss McGrail, and there were a few Physio girls near the counter, and a couple of theatre nurses. I took my tea and bun to the nearest empty table and listened to the Physio girls chattering. It was the usual non-hospital chitchat. Something about a wedding one of them was going to and the suit she'd bought for it. Then I heard one of them say: "The hat you had for Gerry's would do, wouldn't it? Don't you think so, Gerry?"

I looked across quickly. Gerry—and there surely couldn't be two of them in the department—looked rather nice. She was the little fair one, as we usually called her. A bit like Val, but thinner and quieter. She was still there, alone, when Val came in, in mufti, looking for me. I wondered whether to tell her then, but it didn't seem the right moment and I let it pass.

Instead I asked her whether she was going to the dance.

She nodded happily. "Of course. With Sam. And I'm keeping my fingers crossed for the evening. I'm down for one, but Sister Thorpe's quite capable of changing it at the last minute."

"I thought she didn't do that kind of thing," I said. "She's usually considered pretty reasonable, isn't she?"

"She is, normally. But the wind's definitely in the east this week. None of us can do anything right. You know what Staff Bulloughs is like—a place for everything, and everything in its place?"

"Do I not! She nearly drove me mad when I was her night junior last year. Finicky isn't the word. Lord, she had me boiling up all the patients' face-flannels every night and *ironing* the things! Why?"

"Well, she tore a strip off *her* for untidiness."

"Sister did?"

"Uhuh. Now you know the kind of mood she's in, don't you?"

"Fierce, obviously." I put my cup down. "Did you want me for something special, or is this just a social call? Because I'm going across to the Home, now."

"I thought you might come out for a bit. We could go down to the chicken place and eat."

"No Sam?"

"No Sam. He's on call. Are you going out with Peter or anything?"

I pushed my chair under the table and realised as I did so that Gerry Marston was discreetly looking Val over. So she had heard something, I thought. When she saw me watching her she smiled faintly and looked away again. "No," I said. "I'm not going out with Peter. If you'll wait while I change I'll come. But why the chicken place? You haven't been there since——" I stopped because Gerry was still near enough to hear, and urged Val towards the door.

"Since I went with Jock? I know. That's why."

Out on the Main Drag I said: "What do you mean, that's why? Are you out to lay the ghost?"

Val glanced at me to see whether I was laughing at her. "Something like that. I suppose you think that's silly?"

"No. But I should have thought you'd already done that in the Aviary."

"That's where you're wrong. It was at the chicken place that I first spoke to him. . . . He came in alone and said: 'Aren't you from Ward Seven?' That's how it began. . . . It seems such a long time ago, and it can't be more than three months or so. It was at the beginning of this Change."

"Four," I reminded her. "You went to Ward Seven a month before the end of last Change, remember?"

She stopped walking to think for a moment, and then walked on again through the Aviary. "Do you know, I'd forgotten that? Of course . . . it was the end of June. Such a drizzly June, too. Like November, almost."

"Not very long."

"No. But it seems long." She stopped again, by the corner where she'd last sat with Sam, the corner where she'd parted with Jock Marston, too. "I'll wait here for you."

I wondered why she suddenly had the desire to exorcise Jock. But I didn't ask. She would tell me when she was ready.

She was ready, in fact, as soon as we had got through our chicken breasts and French fried, and were watching Ernest pour our second cups of coffee.

She waited until he had gone back to the counter and then pushed the sugar towards me. That made it clear that she was deep in thought, because she knows perfectly well that I don't take sugar in coffee or anything else. It spoils the flavour. "I'm glad I came," she said. "He isn't here any more." She stirred her own cup thoughtfully. "I had to make sure I was over it."

"Don't tell me Sam's proposed to you?"

"No. But he will. It's not that . . . Brownie, I heard only today that Jock's married. Simon James told me."

I nodded. "He told me, too. I couldn't think how to tell you. Or whether I ought to. I nearly did in the canteen this evening."

"That was her, wasn't it?"

"You *knew*? You didn't flicker an eyelash!"

"Well . . . I didn't know that *you* knew, you see. . . . She looks rather nice."

"That's what I thought. . . . You're not fretting, are you?"

She shook her head. "No. It's over. Just like that."

"I'm glad," I said. "Not because of Sam, but because of you."

"It's the same thing."

"I'm glad about that, too. But don't let Sam hurt you. He's never had a real steady before. Maybe it won't be you."

She was so sure. "Yes, it will. I know."

It was a pity that after all that we decided to walk round to the Home by way of the ambulance park. Because this led us straight past Casualty's windows, and some of them were lit. In the little plaster-room leading off minor ops Sam, with his back to the window, was standing close to Miss McGrail. He had both hands on her shoulders, and she was looking up at him the way I must have looked at Frederic and Fairfax.

If Val saw them, too, she didn't say anything. Neither did I. I was wondering all over again whether it had been Dr. Cheshire who had come in when Peter and I were standing together in much the same way. Only I hadn't looked up at Peter like that, I was sure; though whoever had come in wouldn't have been able to see my face.

CHAPTER FIVE

THE Casualty night nurse is a girl named Poulton. She's married, and lives out, and has Saturday and Sunday nights off. On the morning of the dance she looked round the rest of us in the duty-room and said: "Who's doing my week-end?"

Middleman was surprised. "How d'you mean? I thought they had a runner from Ward Ten to answer the bell at weekends."

"Not this week, chum. There's a list of p.p. tonsils of Mr. Arden's. About ten, I think. There'll have to be somebody down here all the time."

Mr. Arden is our E.N.T. man, who comes out from Queen's to operate every few weeks. He doesn't have any bed allocation, and his cases usually spend a couple of nights in the small recovery ward off Casualty.

"There *would* be," Middleman said. "Just because to-night's the dance and every single night nurse who can be spared wants to go to it. I suppose somebody on days'll have to stand in till they come back, that's all. But not this child. My current attraction's coming over specially from R.O.H." Middleman was newly engaged to an Oswestry registrar and couldn't resist plugging the fact at every opportunity. "And Jackson and Grainger both have heavy dates, so they won't do it. How about you, Brownie?"

I was quite firm about it. "I don't know why you think Cinderella's my middle name," I said. "I'm going to the dance, of course. With Peter Stead."

"Oh, well. Sister Rhys-Williams will just have to cope with it as best she can. It's not our worry, after all. And it's not beyond Matron to pressgang somebody, plans or no plans."

"I'd come in myself," Poulton explained, "but Eric's home this weekend, and he'd shoot me down in flames if I spent five minutes away from him. If it had been last week I'd have done it like a shot, while he was up north. I mean, he wouldn't let me do nights at all if he wasn't travelling away so much, so when he *is* here I can't expect to be off the leash, can I?"

The situation was very quickly resolved. I went to early break, so as to get back to Minor Ops in time for Mr. Arden's list, and found Val in the canteen too, in a black mood. "I've been up to office," she told me. "That woman! Well, she's made up my mind for me, I suppose."

"Matron? What's she done to you?"

"Only told me I've to look after the Ts and As until after the dance. Charming! Can't spare a night nurse, and I'm the only one she can use who knows the drill, and who's done the little beasts before."

"Didn't you *tell* her you were booked for the dance?"

"Of course I did! You don't imagine she wanted to know, do you? She said if I could find a substitute all well and good, but it had to be somebody who knew the ropes in case there were any bleeders."

"Look—what did you mean, it had made up your mind for you?"

She sighed and put down her cup with a little bang. "I've been tossing up whether to go or not, as a matter of fact. The McGrail girl's chasing Sam as fast as her legs will carry her, and I've half a mind to give her enough rope to hang herself. If he has to dance with *her* more than twice either he'll be so bored that he'll snub her once and for all or he'll succumb. And if he's going to succumb, the sooner the better."

"You're not mug enough to hand him over just like that, surely?"

"Frankly, I don't think she has a chance. But I'd like her to find that out quickly and leave him alone. See?"

"You're being ridiculous," I grumbled. "If Matron hadn't shoved you on late you'd have gone all right, you know you would. And you've kept her at bay long enough for her to see the light."

"Maybe . . . Yes, I suppose I should. I'm just rationalising because I can't do anything else, I suppose."

"You *can* do something else. You can find a substitute."

"Oh, yes? Well, you tell me, who is there? Who *is* there who knows the drill and who won't mind missing the dance?"

"Is Sister Thorpe on today?"

"No. It's her long weekend. Bulloughs is on."

"Then maybe I'll ring you if I think of anyone. Right?"

"All right."

I left her glooming there and went back to Minor Ops. The ten children were all in bed in the recovery ward, ready to be carried through into the theatre in turn. It always seems tough on the last one, who has to lie there watching the others taken out alive and kicking and brought back a few minutes later half-round and looking pretty messy. They do get a pre-med to keep them quiet, but most of them are still wakeful and don't miss much. But that's the way it's always been done at Thickers, and the best I could do was to steal a couple of screens from O.P. and put them between the beds of the done and the undone, moving them along as we went. Even then it must have been a refined kind of torture for the undone to watch the screens moving nearer and to listen to the gurgles beyond them.

Miss McGrail had come down to anaesthetise and Peter was assisting. In fact, all he had to do was to mop out, and pass things when Mr. Arden didn't snatch them for himself. Like most E.N.T. surgeons, Mr. Arden is large, beefy and dark, rather like a well-dressed butcher, and moves fast. He is apt to grab at instruments as though he had a train to catch, though actually I think he simply likes to get off early to his golf on Saturdays.

He certainly moved fast with those tonsils. I was kept running the whole time, carrying a child in, turning it over to drain, taking it back to bed, moving up the screens, bringing the next in and so on. And when Mr. Arden had scrubbed his big hairy arms and climbed out of his gown into his overpadded jacket and shot off, the three of us were almost out of breath. But I'd had time to think. I said distinctly, for Miss McGrail's benefit: "Peter, I don't think I can come to the dance. I've got to look after this little lot till somebody comes back to relieve me."

He turned round, taking off his red rubber apron, and raised his eyebrows. "But why *you*?"

"Well, it's either me or Val. And Sam'll be terribly disappointed if Val can't go. I can't do that to her. Can I?"

"And what about me? Won't *I* be disappointed?"

"Yes, but——"

"Who am I supposed to take, then?"

"Heavens, there must be dozens of girls who'll be only

too delighted to see you there unattached. How absurd can you be?"

"That's just it. I shan't have you there to fend them off for me."

Miss McGrail giggled. "Well . . . *I* used to play defence at netball. Maybe I could help?"

"Maybe you could, Miss McGrail," I said. "I'm sure you'd make a splendid bodyguard for him." I ignored Peter's expression, walked past him into the ward and went round the children, changing their bowls for clean ones and checking their pulses. While I was doing all that I was still wondering what had made me say it: I had a new dress waiting in my wardrobe, and Hobbs had promised to set my hair.

Peter was wondering too, obviously. After Miss McGrail had clicked away across the hall he came into the ward to me, frowning. "What the hell's got into you? I thought you *liked* dancing with me. You always——"

"I do," I confessed quickly. "Very much. You know that darned well. But that wretched girl's pursuing Sam, and if Val isn't there tonight to watch over him there's no knowing what might happen. See?"

"What girl? Mary McGrail? That's just too silly: she sees him all the time in quarters, so what difference will one evening make?"

Peter was not very perceptive about things like atmosphere. But then, I decided, very few men were. "What difference? Quite a lot," I said. "Over in quarters she doesn't have the opportunity to lure him into the Aviary, does she? No soft lights and sweet music over there, either. What's more, if Val's in possession at the dance, for everyone to see, she may accept the fact that he's hooked and leave him alone. . . . I mean, Val can't just go up to her in the ward and say, 'Lay off Sam, or else,' can she? But at the dance she can say it without words, as it were."

"I see." Peter folded his long arms on the end of a bed and watched me mopping up a toddler's bloodstained face.

"I see. You want me to act decoy, is that it? . . . Defence at netball; I ask you!"

"Yes, please." I smiled back at the little girl and winked to reassure her. "Go to sleep, now, there's a good girl. . . . Yes, that's just what I do want." I turned the smile on to Peter.

"You don't want much, do you?" Then he relaxed. "Well—for you, I'll do it. On condition."

I tucked in the blankets and moved on to the next bed with my swab tray. "What condition?" I said. "Chuck me that towel, Peter, there's a dear."

He put the towel in my hand and squeezed my wrist. "On condition you come out with me on your half-day next week."

"I'll consider it," I promised lightly.

"Good." He patted the back of my belt possessively. "I'll hold you to it." At the door he looked back. "I'll bet she can't even dance," he said gloomily. "Netball, indeed!"

"It was defence she played," I reminded him. "Not attack. You can always sit out. Unless you still fancy the red-head?"

I told Val at lunchtime, because I hadn't had a split second to ring her. "It's O.K. You don't have to stay on. I've found somebody."

"Somebody who's done it before?"

"Yes."

"Somebody senior enough?"

"Yes."

"Somebody who *will*?"

"Yes."

"Then who? Because I've racked my brains."

"Me," I said smugly. "And don't make a speech about it. Peter doesn't mind."

"Oh, Brownie! No, I won't let you. You know you were looking forward to it. Don't be ridiculous."

"I told you not to make a speech," I warned her. "You're

going. And if you let the McGrail girl get past you you're dimmer than I thought you were. Now shut up and pass me the mint sauce before they filter all the mint out of it."

I met Sam along the Main Drag on my way back to O.P. It was the first time I'd seen him to speak to since the night Val and I had gone to the chicken restaurant. "Be good tonight," I said. "I shan't be there to keep you in line."

"Why on earth not?"

"Late duty," I explained. "Mr. Arden's kids. Oh—by the way, Sam, do be tactful. I think Peter's got a thing about Miss McGrail, and I'm pretty sure she has about him, too. So don't you go cutting in, or you may get a thick ear." I thought that was pretty clever of me. "Now watch it, Sam!"

He stared at me. "Well . . . thanks for the tip, mate. You just never know your luck, do you? That's rough. I'd have sworn old Peter was completely pro-you. Funny."

"You don't know him. A girl in every ward, that's Peter. Or was, till now."

Sam nodded slowly. "Till now, yes. But when he told me he'd suddenly become one-track I honestly thought he meant you. I could have sworn . . . So it's *la* McGrail, after all? You could have fooled me! Don't you *mind*?"

"Not a bit," I assured him. "Peter's really not my type."

He still looked surprised as he wandered away. For a young man who spends a good deal of his time in thinking up elaborate practical jokes for future use Sam is astonishingly gullible.

It seemed to me that I had done pretty well for Val. The glow of conscious virtue I got from it very nearly made up for the glow I wasn't going to get from dancing with Peter. It wasn't until a good deal later that it occurred to me that he and Mary McGrail might in fact get on a good deal better than I anticipated, and then I felt like kicking myself for being so quixotic.

If I put my head out through the plaster-room window I could hear the dance-band quite plainly across the lawns. I was standing on the big plaster bin with my chin on the edge of the windowsill when Val came across to see me, through the back door.

I climbed down. "You'll get shot if Sister Rhys-Williams catches you," I said. She looked smashing, I told her, in her blue lurex sheath dress.

"Sister Rhys-Williams is too busy," she assured me. "Chasing all the men at the rate of knots."

"Yes, and giggling," I agreed. "I know. You *are* a mug to leave Sam. What possessed you?"

"I didn't. He left me, to go to the phone, so I came to see how you were."

"I'm fine. What's Peter doing?"

"Clumping round with Miss McGrail." She began to laugh. "He looks so bored, poor lamb."

"Well, don't tell Sam so. I've given him the notion that this thing is bigger than both of them and that he'd better keep out."

She looked at me curiously. "Now why did you—oh, I see. Very clever. But it's only too obvious that any minute now Peter's going to escape and play havoc among the juniors. . . . I must say some of the first-years really are smashers when they get their war-paint on. You never saw so much eye-shadow in your life."

"Ah, they won't need it when they're our age. We just naturally get rings round our eyes," I said. "And I suppose the Big Cheese is stepping out with Staff Williams?"

"Dr. Cheshire? Is he, scissors! He isn't even there."

I blinked. "Not *there*? But he bought two tickets. Maybe he's been delayed."

"Maybe. . . . I'd better fly back now, before the Stead–McGrail axis disintegrates."

I saw her out, and turned off the plaster-room light before I went back to the ward. I thought I had locked the door after her, but I couldn't have done, because I heard it open and close again half an hour later and nobody had come through the front way. For a moment I didn't react: I was more interested in the little boy in the end bed. There was no doubt about it: I had a bleeder on my hands. The thin trickle of bright blood that I'd been keeping tabs on was persisting. I snapped off my torch and went through to the telephone, and then I re-registered the door sounds. Dr. Cheshire was sitting on the desk. He looked fabulous in tails.

"Good evening, Nurse," he said, not smiling. "And why are you still on duty?"

"Somebody had to be, sir." I reached round him for the telephone. "Excuse me. I've got a bleeder. I'd better get somebody down to put a post-nasal plug in."

"Can't you do it yourself?"

"Naturally. But for some reason we're not supposed to."

"What rubbish! Go ahead. I'll be responsible. I can't do it myself with this confounded finger. I'll come and watch."

I hesitated. He couldn't really take the responsibility. Mr. Arden's tonsils were clean out of his province. But after all, he was a qualified man. And any fool can put a p.n. plug in. Even me. "All right, sir," I agreed. I pushed the phone back in its place again. "If you say so. They can't do more than shoot me, I suppose."

He followed me idly while I collected a fine catheter and some strapping, and fished out a sterile plug from the jar on the trolley. "Adrenalin?" I asked. "We usually do, while we're at it."

He nodded. "Surely. Carry on."

He leaned on the end of the bed and brooded over me while I threaded the oiled catheter into the little boy's nose. Most children kick up—and who shall blame them?—but this one was an angel.

"I know what you're doing," he volunteered thickly, when I turned to souse the plug in the gallipot of adrenalin. "You're sending down a sort of ferret to bring the tape up." He swallowed manfully. "Aren't you?"

"How right you are!" I was surprised, to say the least. "And how did you know?"

"My Mummy said you might have to. She said I had to let you, and it would be O.K. if I kept swallowing."

"Well, good for your mummy," I told him. "Was she a nurse?"

He nodded, and opened wide for me to reach the catheter with the long forceps. When I'd fastened the tape on to it he said: "This is the worst bit, isn't it?"

"Pulling the tape through? Yes, I suppose it is. But it won't take two ticks . . . keep breathing; big breaths, old dear." He was very good. Thirty seconds later I was strapping the tapes to his jaw. "Well done, you," I congratulated him. "You can tell your mummy you behaved beautifully." I turned to Dr. Cheshire and held out my throat torch. "You want to check, sir?"

He took a perfunctory look. "Fine," he agreed. "Nicely done. That should fix him." He pushed his fist gently against the little boy's chin. "All right, cobber. Go to sleep now. All right?"

I tidied the bed and took the tray away, and he followed me back to the steriliser. I looked at him over my shoulder. "Did you want something, sir?" He seemed very much at a loose end.

He shrugged. "I thought I'd get this finger redressed. If you can spare the time. It's fairly painful still."

"Of course." I could have kicked myself. "I didn't think."

When it was done and I was spinning the tubular gauze over the dressing he said: "So you don't care for dancing?"

"On the contrary, sir, I'm very fond of it. Given the right partner, of course."

"Of course."

He twinkled at me, and it emboldened me to ask: "Aren't you going yourself, sir?"

"I was. But not now. For one thing I seem to be wearing the wrong clothes. For another, I don't have a partner."

I turned away to put the thimble back on the trolley. "Well, I admit white ties aren't usual, at our hops. Not that it matters. You can please yourself, surely?" I wanted to say, "You look so marvellous that nobody would mind a bit," but that would never have done. "As to not having a partner, well, you don't need one, sir. There are loads of spare girls."

"I don't want a 'spare girl'." He sounded almost irritable. "I'd hoped to——"

"Oh, your partner let you down, sir?"

"That's about it." He got off the table where he'd been sitting and pulled his cuffs straight. "She couldn't come."

I switched on the steriliser and dropped in the gallipots and forceps I'd been using, wondering who "she" could be.

"She couldn't come," he repeated. "Seems she got stuck with some tonsil kids, or something."

I swung round and stared at him. "She—she *what*?"

"Well, didn't you?"

"*Me?*"

"Obviously." He was smiling faintly, but when I went on staring the smile faded and he frowned. "You had my note, surely?"

"Note? No, sir. Besides——"

"Besides, you wouldn't have come anyway?"

I felt my face getting red. "Well, how could I, sir? You're a consultant, and——"

"Oh, tommyrot! *Didn't* you get the note? Seriously?"

"Seriously."

"That's queer. I stuck it in the front office for you."

"And how was it addressed?"

"Well, just 'Nurse Brown'. I don't know the rest."

"That explains it," I said. "There are two other Browns, both senior to me. And one's on holiday."

"What should I have put?"

"It doesn't matter. I couldn't have come, anyway. But it was kind of you, all the same."

"Kind?" He came over and stood in front of me, and tipped my chin up with his finger. "Hardly. I just thought you'd be a nice sort of person to dance with. I *can* dance. They had me properly taught when I was in my teens. I wouldn't have trodden on your feet or anything. . . . Come here." He took my elbow and ran me out on to the paving outside the back door. "Listen."

I listened. The band was playing a slow waltz. It was one of my favourites, as it happened, an old one called *Moonlight Madonna*, which has always had a devastating effect on me. "Yes," I said, as casually as I could. "It's a sin the way they murder the classics by turning them into dance tunes, isn't it?"

He held out his arms. "Let me prove that I can dance."

Maybe the tune, or the quiet moonlight, paralysed my common sense momentarily. I don't know. I do know that we floated and weaved across the paved square as elegantly as if it had been a sprung floor laid there for the purpose. It was quite an experience. He was as adept as Peter, and a good deal lighter on his feet. And there was a lot more to it than that, only I didn't want to admit it. So when the music stopped and he let me go I said: "Sir, really! I *must* go in. This is idiotic."

"But nice," he said softly "Wasn't it?" He looked very tall against the moonlit wall. "Wasn't it?"

I remembered to breathe. "Yes," I admitted. "Very. Good night, sir."

I turned and ran. When I had locked the back door behind me I leaned against it for a long time, waiting for my pulse to quieten down, before I went round the children again. The little boy with the plug was asleep, and at the foot of his bed something white lay crumpled on the red blanket. A dressing towel that I'd dropped, I thought. I picked it up as I passed. When I got back to the light again I looked at it. It wasn't a dressing towel at all, but a clean white handkerchief with one of those red woven labels saying *Cheshire*. It must have fallen out of his sleeve as he leaned there. It had a faintly spicy smell; not a perfume, just a tang. Something like a mixture of Harris tweed and expensive cigars. It had the same effect on me as *Moonlight Madonna*, and I tucked it away quickly behind my apron bib. It was no time to indulge in sentiment. I was on duty. When Sister Rhys-Williams pattered in, still buttoning her sleeves, I was finishing a brief report.

She frowned down at it. "What's this? Post-nasal plug inserted? By whom?"

"Well—actually, I did it, Sister."

"Oh, you did, did you, Nurse? And since when has that been allowed? You know perfectly well you should have rung for a houseman, don't you? Even *I* wouldn't put a plug in without asking somebody. Well?" Her eyes were at their beadiest.

"I know, Sister . . . Well, Dr. Cheshire was here, and he said——"

"Dr. Cheshire? Huh! What does *he* know about E.N.T. cases?"

I would have liked to tell her that he probably knew a good deal more about them than a raw houseman, but it would hardly have been politic. I said: "I'm sorry, Sister."

"You *will* be, Nurse. You *will* be. Because Matron will hear about this. . . ." She went over it all again, and broke off only when the night nurse, still sporting her lipstick and eye-shadow, hurried in. "Ah, Nurse Mayne. It takes you a long time to change, doesn't it? *I've* been here for at least ten minutes."

When she had gone Mayne looked at me. "What upset *her* apple-cart?"

"She can't have had the right partners," I said. "All that was because I put a p.n. plug in."

"Oh, sucks. We've all done that before now. You can't go dragging housemen out of bed just for that. . . . As for not having the right partners, I don't think she had any at all, actually. Except the lab. boy—and she only managed to grab him in a Paul Jones." She hung up her cape and took her cuffs off, and pulled her soft night slippers out of her case. "Oh, one thing . . . who do you think came sailing in, all got up regardless, white tie and everything?"

"I can't imagine." I moved over to the door. "Who?"

"Dr. Cheshire of all people. Now there's a man. A real man."

It was absurd, I knew, but I felt a niggling little pang of jealousy. "Oh? Did you get a dance with him?"

"What, me? Not likely. Nobody did, as a matter of fact. He came in, looked round, spoke to Peter Stead and vanished. Oh, we weren't nearly grand enough for him, my dear. . . . I bet he's a good dancer, too," she mused.

She was right there. "Could be," I said. "Could be. Well, I'm off." I walked her round the ward and then left her to it. I was tired.

I expected to find Val waiting for me, in my room or hers, but she wasn't. Both rooms were empty. Maybe, I thought, she was still saying good night to Sam. Or maybe she was taking a late bath. At any rate I was much too sleepy to hang around waiting for her to return to base. And I was much too occupied with the things that were surging around in my head. I lay flat on my back, after I had turned out the light, and went right through that waltz again, out on the moonlit paving behind the O.P. block. It was quite something: the hardness of Dr. Cheshire's forearm behind me; the spicy tang that I'd recognised on his handkerchief; the feel of his muscular shoulder under my left palm, and the dreamy long-legged confidence of his dancing. I couldn't even think about dancing with Peter in the same breath—and that was a shock. A real shock. Until then that had been just about my "most rewarding experience", as the T.V. shows called it. It had never occurred to me that there was anything that could have the edge over that. Evidently I had been wrong.

I turned over and lay with my face in my pillow, and danced it through again for the third time. It was at some point during this process that I remembered the handkerchief lying on my dressing-table, where I'd dropped it as I undressed. I slipped out of bed to reach for it, and went to sleep with it under my mouth.

I tucked it behind my apron bib again when I dressed next morning. It was childish, perhaps, but it was something I wanted to do, and I did it. Several times during the morning, between tonsil-mopping and dealing with stray casualties, I took it out and buried my face in it. I was doing just that when Sam shot in unexpectedly.

"Got a cold?" he said. "Poor old Sis."

"That's right," I agreed. "A cold. And how are you, after the dance? You kept Val out late enough, didn't you?"

He stared at me. "I like that! *I* kept Val out. I never set eyes on her after about ten o'clock. Did she clear off to bed, or what?"

I thought that one over. Val certainly hadn't been in bed at midnight. On the other hand, it seemed hardly politic to say so. "Yes," I said. "Probably. Actually I've not seen her yet today—I was late for breakfast."

"Slack devil," Sam commented. "Well, when you do see her——"

"You'll see her first," I pointed out. "You'll be doing a ward-round, surely?"

"But she isn't *on*. I've been up there. And everybody was remarkably cagey about it."

I turned to stare at him then. "Isn't *on*? Then where is she?"

"I haven't a clue. That's why I'm asking."

It was ridiculous. Thickers was a hospital, a perfectly normal hospital. People didn't just disappear. . . .

"I'll check at lunchtime," I suggested feebly. "All right?"

"All right," Sam began to laugh. "I say, you were going it a bit, weren't you? Dancing with the Big Cheese out in the garden. *Danse Macabre* if ever I saw it."

"I don't know what you mean," I said.

"Come off it, Sis. You were enjoying it. You looked properly sent."

"Shut up," I told him. "Don't be ridiculous."

"Well, you did. Mary said——"

I turned my head sharply. "Mary? You mean Miss McGrail?"

"Clever, these Chinese! That's right. Mary McGrail. She said——"

"I don't care *what* she said," I told him firmly. "And for heaven's sake get out of my hair. I'm busy." I picked up a bowlful of swabs and pushed past him. "Mary McGrail can go and tie herself in reef-knots as far as I'm concerned."

It was just too bad that she was standing in the doorway listening. And the way she was looking at Sam really had me worried. Worried about Val, as much as anything. If I hadn't had that handkerchief to finger behind my apron bib I don't think I could have lasted out till lunchtime.

CHAPTER SIX

STAFF WILLIAMS thrust me aside with her dry, pointed elbow and smoothly took over the Colles' plaster I was finishing. "You're to go to Matron," she said, in a distant kind of voice. "*Now.*" She didn't look at me.

It was no more than I had expected, but just to stall I said: "What for, I wonder?"

Mary McGrail, perched on her stool by the anaesthetic machine, positively sniggered. I remembered then what Sam had said, and I treated her to what I hoped was a sizzling glare as I rinsed my hands.

"*Now,*" Staff Williams repeated. "And don't forget your cuffs, Nurse." She looked so smug that I wanted to hit her, and I wondered just how much she knew about it. She smiled faintly at Miss McGrail and added, at me: "It doesn't do to keep Matron waiting. It only makes things worse."

By the time I reached the office and tapped on the door I was dithering. And the loud mannish "Come!" didn't help. All the same, when I went in and stood in front of the big desk Matron didn't look angry in the least. She was worried, though. Very worried. She kept twisting her College of Nursing medallion on its chain until I thought she would have it snap clean off before she said anything. It seemed up to me to start the conversational ball rolling, so I said: "You sent for me, Matron." Not a very bright remark, but at least it jolted her out of her trance.

"Yes. Yes, Nurse, I did. . . . Tell me—you're a close friend of Nurse Ringway's?"

I nodded. "Well, yes, Matron." What had that to do with moonlight waltzes in the car-park? "We were in the same P.T.S. set," I elaborated, "and we've been pretty close ever since."

"Then perhaps you can tell me where she is?" Her stony eyes had anxious puckers round them. "Or where she might be? Can you?"

"Where she *is*, Matron?" I was puzzled. You couldn't simply mislay a nurse. Not at Thickers. "I—I don't know what you mean," I said. "Has she—has she disappeared or something?"

"Or something, as you say, Nurse. . . . I gather that Nurse was last seen shortly after ten o'clock, at the monthly dance. Have you any idea at all of her movements since then?"

I thought about it. Val certainly hadn't been in her room at midnight. I said so. "But I went straight to bed, myself," I explained, "so I can't really tell you anything, Matron."

"And this morning?"

"I was—well, I was in rather a rush, Matron. I didn't see her, I'm afraid."

"And this didn't strike you as unusual?"

I frowned. "I did wonder where she was, yes, Matron."

"But you didn't see fit to report that she was missing?"

Missing sounded quite different from simply not being around. "It didn't occur to me, Matron," I admitted. "I mean, it was just that I didn't happen to see her, and——"

"Well, Nurse, she must be found. And we literally have

no idea where she went after ten o'clock last night. Now tell me—was Nurse Ringway at all unhappy here?"

We all groused at times, I said. You couldn't call that being actively *unhappy*. "Besides," I went on, "if there was anything worrying her she'd have told me."

"Quite, Nurse. That was what I assumed. And did she?"

Matron looked at me searchingly. I got the impression that she was studying my cerebellar structure in detail. "*Did* she tell you something was worrying her?"

There was always Sam, I reflected. And Mary McGrail. But Matron wouldn't see that kind of thing as a worry. In any case Val wasn't the sort to go off into a fugue or anything just because her love-life didn't go according to Millicent Ashdown, as we say. "No, Matron," I said firmly. "No, she didn't."

Matron sighed. "Very well, Nurse. Then I'm reluctantly forced to the conclusion that I'd better inform the police." This prospect obviously filled her with the acutest distaste. "You're absolutely sure you can't suggest anything?"

"I can't," I said helplessly. "I can't think of a single reason why she should go adrift, Matron."

"Do you know of anyone else who might?"

There was Sam, of course, but I was quite sure he would be as baffled as I was. I shook my head. "I'm sorry, Matron. I can't think of anyone right now. But of course I'll make some enquiries."

"When are you off duty, Nurse?" Still no word of my atrocious behaviour by moonlight.

I thought quickly. "Probably this evening, Matron. It usually is, in O.P."

"Yes, I see, Nurse. Would it help at all if I asked Sister to release you early?"

"It might, Matron. But I hope you'll have heard something before then."

She dropped the twisted medallion chain and let both her hands fall heavily to the desk. They lay on the leather like the talons of a dying eagle. "Yes, Nurse. So do I. So do I."

The talons were clamped round the telephone when I left her.

Sister Branker was bulging with curiosity. "I hear your friend's missing, Nurse," she breathed. "Were you able to help at all?"

"No, Sister," I confessed. "I simply haven't a clue. It's so odd she should just vanish, like that. I mean, she came——" I stopped. It wasn't really wise.

Sister Branker's eyebrows went up. "Well? She came over to see you, did she?"

She was rather a dear: there wasn't much point in being cagey with her. "Well, actually, yes. Ninish, I suppose it would be. She was happy enough, then. . . . You know, Sister, I've a horrid feeling she's gone and got herself locked in a cupboard or something."

"Yes, but that's silly. The Home's been thoroughly searched, Nurse. Wherever she may be she most certainly isn't on the premises, I can assure you. . . . But Home Sister says that none of her outdoor clothes seem to have gone."

It was more than Matron had told me, I reflected. I said: "That just goes to show that this wasn't something she'd planned. . . . But she can't have been *spirited* away, can she?" Then I thought of something. It was rather silly, but it was a point. "There isn't anyone else missing, is there, Sister?"

"Not that I know of. A man, you mean?"

Sister Branker would. That hadn't occurred to me, and I told her so.

"Well, it's possible," she declared. "People *do* run off together sometimes, Nurse. I mean, you *read* about these things happening, let's face it."

I agreed. "But not Nurse Ringway, Sister. She wouldn't. At least, I don't think she would, not without my seeing the possibility, if you see what I mean."

"Matron says that if you want any extra time, Nurse . . ."

"It's all right, Sister. All I really can do is to talk to some of the people who were at the dance." I looked at the rapidly filling hall. "Do you want me to do dressings, Sister?"

"Yes. You may as well. There really oughtn't to be so many on a Sunday, ought there? But there was that glass business, and . . ." She looked dreamily over my shoulder. "You don't think this is some—some *prank*, do you? Some of the students . . . well, you know what they are, Nurse."

"Were there any at the dance?"

"Oh, yes. Quite a few. A bit wild, I thought."

I shrugged off that idea as soon as she had gone. Val wasn't the sort to be larking about with students, not when Sam was around anyhow. All the same, the whole thing was very odd.

The police came at tea-time. There was a plain-clothes man waiting for me in the hall when I went off duty. He stepped forward, tall and dark, in a raincoat, from the alcove by the front office, and said: "Nurse Brown? Detective-sergeant Pallett. About Nurse Ringway . . ."

"Your guess is as good as mine," I said flatly. "I have no ideas at all. Didn't Matron——"

"Matron said I could talk to you. All right? I suppose we couldn't get a cup of tea?"

I took him along to the canteen. The looks we got were like arrows in my back, but I was past caring about that. "Look," I said. "This is the basic point: she was at the dance with a—with a chap she's very fond of. As far as I know they didn't squabble or anything. So why should she just walk out?"

He shook his head and put four lumps of sugar in his tea. "Girls do queer things. And they *did* squabble, you know."

"Oh?"

"Yes. Dr. Brown tells me there were a few words."

It was more than Sam had told me, and I was cross with him for leaving me in the dark.

"I don't suppose it was anything serious," I protested.

"Maybe not. . . . Put yourself in her shoes: where would *you* flounce off to?"

"Bed," I said promptly. "Where else is there? Anyhow, she didn't, did she?"

He threw a list across the table at me. "People at the dance," he explained. "Have I missed any?"

"How would I know? I wasn't there." I ran my finger down the list just the same. "*He* wasn't," I pointed out.

He twisted his head to look. "Dr. Cheshire? I heard he was. He had tickets, I'm told."

"Yes, but I think he just put his head in and left right away. He didn't really *go* to the thing."

"Hm." He looked at me under his lashes.

"What does that mean?"

"Nobody seems to know where he is, either."

I looked up quickly, startled. "How d'you mean?"

"He isn't here; he isn't at his flat, and the woman who cleans for him says he should be. Somebody reckoned they both left the dance round the same time."

That, I knew, wasn't true. "You're not suggesting——"

"Not suggesting anything. But there it is."

I stood up and pushed my chair sharply under the table. We were getting nowhere, fast. "I'm sorry," I said. "I really don't know anything. If you'll excuse me . . .?"

His pencil across the back of my wrist restrained me gently. "One more thing. What was she wearing?"

It was an odd question. I'd always imagined that a description was the first thing the police asked for when a missing person was reported, and I said so. "Didn't Matron——?"

"She did. Just checking." He smiled quickly. "Routine, as we say."

The idea of anyone checking any statement of Matron's struck me as highly unsuitable, but I supposed that in his job even she was just one more witness. "A blue affair," I told him. "Lurex, you know. It's a sort of metallic——"

"I know. My wife has a blouse. . . . Long or short?"

"Short. What we call a sheath dress."

He nodded and scribbled. Evidently his wife had one of those, too. I noticed that he was rather good-looking, and compared him mentally with Andy Crawford of Dock Green. "Nothing else? I mean, a wrap or something?"

"I don't think so."

"Hm. Not exactly hiking kit."

"No," I agreed. "That's why I——"

"Not to worry." He stood up, snapping the elastic band round his notebook. "She'll turn up. They usually do, you know."

It was then, hearing Val classified as "they", as one of the disappearing girls who were obviously so much routine to Detective-sergeant Pallett, that I began to worry in earnest. Where *was* Val? Surely something unthinkable must have happened to her? What was more, where was Dr. Cheshire? And had something—either the same thing or something quite different—happened to him, too?

Ernest came and took away the chicken and chips eventually, when I'd been staring at the plate for more than half an hour. "Not hungry, Miss? Another cup of coffee, then?" I suppose he was used to dealing with people who'd been stood up, because he added: "It's the traffic, you know. Something chronic it is, in the evenings. People get delayed."

I didn't explain that I was merely waiting for my brother, and that he had only the length of a couple of wards to walk. I didn't have to. He came blundering in while Ernest was still saying: "With cream, this time?"

"Make it two," I said. I looked coldly at Sam. "I like your 'right away'," I grumbled. "I've been here——"

"I know, Sis." He sat down and looked apologetic. "Only I got hung up with the Addison's woman."

"Mrs. Andrews? How is she?" I enquired perfunctorily.

"All right now. Gave me a bit of a scare, though." He

watched Ernest frothing up the milk at the counter and waited while he brought our cups over. "Why the royal command, anyway? You can think yourself lucky I took time out."

"Val," I said. "Aren't *you* worried?"

"Not *worried*, no. A bit irritated, really. Police and all that jazz. I mean, she never struck me as the silly sort." He spooned sugar into his cup without looking at me.

"She isn't!" I must have pretty well shouted it, because Ernest turned to look at me from behind the Espresso machine, and blinked. I lowered my voice to a vehement growl. "That's the whole point, you fathead. Something frightful must have happened to her. She *wouldn't* just——" Then I remembered what I'd meant to ask him. "You told the policeman you'd 'had words', he said. What about?"

"Oh, that. It was nothing. . . . There was a ladies' excuse-me thing, and she went chasing off after Simon James, that's all. My *amour propre* was a bit punctured."

"It was?" I was furious with him. "What did you expect her to do if you were hanging round the McGrail girl?" I warmed to this idea. "And how do you think *her* amour-whatsaname felt when she saw you cuddling the wretched woman the other night?"

Sam was genuinely shocked. "*Cuddling?* What, me? You must be off your rocker."

"I was there too," I pointed out. "There you stood in the plaster-room. . . . Gawping into one another's eyes, and——"

He laughed out loud. "So that's it? Eyes being the operative word. She had a chip of plaster in her eye, that's all."

"And I've heard that one before," I said rudely. "It didn't look very clinical to me. Or to Val." All the same, I knew he was speaking the truth. I knew my Sam. I knew too, that Simon James at least hadn't vanished. I had seen him two or three times during the day, flitting round the corridors. "So you squabbled about Simon? Then what?"

"Then nothing. She whisked out and I didn't see her again."

"Just like that?"

"Just like that." He tossed off the rest of his coffee. "She's probably sulking somewhere."

"For twenty-four hours? Don't be clueless." Sam had some crazy ideas about nurses if he thought they could—or would—slide off for a good sulk when there was work to be done, even if they'd dare, which was another thing.

He spread his hands. "That's just what I *am*. Honestly, I *don't* have any clues. You know her a darn sight better than I do. What's your theory?"

I didn't answer him, because at that moment Coralie Lawson sauntered in, with a man in tow. It wasn't anyone I knew, and I didn't think she knew him very well, either, to judge from the way she was simmering at him, in a speculative sort of way, as though she were plumbing the possibilities. And when he said, "Well, now, Miss Lawson . . ." that clinched it.

"Call me Coralie," she suggested. Then she noticed us, sitting in the corner, and bent forward to whisper something in his ear that made him glance across.

He seemed even more interested in me than he was in Coralie, and when I followed Sam out he watched me all the way to the door.

Sam said: "What's the fellow staring at?" He is as uncomplimentary as anyone's brother. "Do you know him?"

"No." I looked back through the net curtains of the restaurant window. "I don't think he knows *la* Lawson either, if you ask me. I wonder who he is?"

"Maybe that's his car?" Sam stopped to look at the shabby little saloon parked outside. There were several crumpled copies of the local rag on the back seat, and on the windscreen there was a PRESS notice that looked as though it had been cut from the title page of the *Daily Express*.

"A reporter? But why?"

He shrugged. "Maybe she's entered for the beauty queen contest or something."

"With those legs? Hardly." Then it hit me. "You *don't* think it could be something to do with Val? That would explain why he was giving us the once-over, wouldn't it?"

Sam stopped walking and turned to look at me uncertainly. "Could be, I suppose. If they're on to it. . . . Shall I go back and shut him up?"

"That would be just about the best way of making sure he prints something, I should think. No, don't, Sam. Leave it alone, for heaven's sake. Coralie doesn't know anything—she's just courting publicity. She's *like* that. If you go and butt in he'll start quizzing you, and then . . . No, don't. Besides, it may be nothing of the kind. Maybe she's simply picked him up. I tell you, she *does* that kind of thing. She's run through most of the Thickers talent; now she's starting to spread her net a bit farther afield, that's all. Leave her to it."

He slid his arm into mine as we walked back to hospital. "I do hope Val *is* all right," he murmured. "You don't think . . .?"

"No. They always turn up," I assured him. "The detective said so. There's probably some perfectly simple explanation. It's just that we haven't thought of it. She'll probably have turned up by the time we get back, you juggins."

But she hadn't.

There was no news next morning, either. And then at ten o'clock, when I was up to my ears in dressings, Staff Williams came to me, very annoyed, and said: "Nurse Brown, you're wanted on the phone. You know perfectly well you're not supposed to have private calls when you're on duty."

"All right, Staff," I said reasonably. "Ask them to ring again when I'm off. I'll be in the Home."

"I told him that." She sniffed. "But he insisted. . . . Of course, it may be the police."

"Him?" I passed her a bandage and moved aside. "This is an old mastoid. I've cleaned it up, but it ought to come in again." I grinned at the child sitting on the table. "If it's the police I'd getter go, then. Maybe there's some news."

I went through to the duty-room phone. "Yes?" I said. "Nurse Brown speaking."

It certainly wasn't Pallett. It wasn't the police at all. All I knew was that it was a male voice, a rather pleasant voice that I felt I'd heard somewhere before. It said: "I have a message from Nurse Ringway for you."

"Nurse Ringway?" I swallowed. "Where *is* she?"

The man laughed softly. "Wouldn't you love to know? That isn't the point. . . . She needs some clothes. She wants you to get them for her, from her room. A day dress and some shoes, and a coat of some kind. All right?"

If I had had any sense at all I would have scribbled: *Trace this call* on the nearest slip of paper, thrown it at someone and kept him talking. But there was nobody around—everyone was working full tilt—and it didn't enter my head until later in any case. I am not used to cloak-and-dagger stuff. Instead I said: "But is she all right? We've been frightfully worried about her."

"She's all right. Not too good-tempered, though. And she's cold. So what about those clothes?"

"What—where am I to bring them?" Even if I can get them, I thought, because her room's sure to be locked. "What is it you want me to do?"

"Just get the clothes. Pack them in something, and I'll get in touch with you again. And don't tell anyone, or else."

"Or else what?"

"Just 'or else'," he said pleasantly. "Got the idea?"

I said I thought I had. Then I asked the most idiotic question of all. "Who are you?"

He rang off.

Back in Dressings I beckoned to the next patient, and got on. I could see that Staff Williams was itching to ask, "Well, was it the police?" so I didn't look her way, except to murmur, "I'm back now, Staff," before I plunged into the work again.

The man whose septic arm I was dressing looked up at me curiously. "You're very quiet this morning, Nurse?"

"Am I? I was thinking."

"Not about anything very pleasant, that's for sure, if your face is any guide!"

"I was just wondering . . . is that too hot? . . . You know how it is when people say: 'Don't tell a soul'? Well, it simply makes you want to rush off and tell the first person you see, doesn't it?"

"Me, say?" He winced as he settled his arm in the arm-bath. "Go on, then."

"No. Not you. But my brother wouldn't count, would he?"

"I shouldn't think so. I reckon when people say that they know darn well you'll tell your family, like. They mean don't tell outsiders, don't they?"

"Or the police?"

"Well, or the police, yes."

"Good," I said. "That's what I wanted to think." I looked round the department. The queue was thinning, and Staff Williams was putting her cuffs on again. "Time I went and had my morning snorter," I told him. "You just stay here and soak till I come back. If it cools off, ask one of the others to fill you up, will you?"

I grabbed my own cuffs and went through to tell Sister it seemed to be a good moment for coffee, if that was all right with her, and bolted for the Home telephone. It took them ages to locate Sam, and when they did he was in a hurry. I explained as fast as I could.

"You'll have to tell the cops," he said. "Didn't you get *any* inkling what it was all about?"

"None at all. But whatever it is, and wherever she is, and whatever she's up to, she's going to need her clothes. So I may as well do what the man said, and pack them."

Sam sighed. "Look, I'm all scrubbed, and Staff Horrocks is holding the receiver for me. You do choose some moments. I'll get on to you later. All right?"

"All right," I said. And then I raced along to Val's room. I'd expected it to be locked, or sealed by the police, or something, and it wouldn't have surprised me in the least if there had been a policeman sitting on a hard chair right outside the door. But I was lucky. The door was unlocked, and so was Val's wardrobe. I took down her pink wool jersey dress, and her grey coat and shoes, and shoved them into an empty weekend case under my own bed. Then I went back to my dressings.

It did occur to me that I ought to go and spill the beans to Matron, to say nothing of ringing Detective-sergeant Pallett, but quite apart from the ethics of the situation, there simply wasn't time. And I heard nothing from Sam until he came down with Mr. Franks to take Dr. Cheshire's clinic, which I'd set for—wondering whether Dr. Cheshire would turn up or not, and pretty sure in my own mind that he wouldn't.

I was quite right. He didn't. Mr. Franks took over the inner room, and Sam coped outside. When there was a lull Sam came across to me with a handful of path. forms and said: "See to these, will you?. . . Have you got on to the cops yet?"

"Not yet. There hasn't been time, actually. I wonder what 'or else' meant?"

"Just bluff, if you ask me. How are they to know you've told anyone?" He had something there.

"Oughtn't I to wait till I get my instructions?"

"Yes. Yes, I suppose that's sense. . . . Look, we'll have to get on. Franks'll be blowing his top if we don't. Keep in touch, won't you?"

The next time Mr. Franks was free I put my head in before I fetched the patient through. "Isn't Dr. Cheshire coming?"

He shrugged. "Apparently not. We've had no message.

He must have got tied up in the traffic. I hear there were a few diversions up that way."

"Up what way?"

"He intended to go fishing, I believe. Some place in North Wales. Didn't he?"

I said: "I've really no idea, Mr. Franks. How would I know what consultants do with their spare time? Are you ready for this query thyroid?"

He was, he said, and would I please push them through a bit faster, or we'd never get done before midnight.

Next time I went out into the hall I ran into Simon James, and simultaneously had a brainwave. I gave him my best smile and hoped it would work. "Simon," I said. "Just the man I want. Look—are you doing anything this evening? Going out anywhere, I mean."

He shook his head. "Afraid I'm second on. Got to stay in till ten. Why?"

"I was wondering. . . . Do you think I could possibly have your car for an hour or so? Not for long. I promise I'll look after it. Truly."

"Of course. I take it you do have a driving licence?. . . Here's the key."

I could have hugged him. "That's sweet of you," I said. "Remind me to do something for you sometime. I'm awfully grateful. I'll explain later."

"Do that. . . . By the way, any news of Nurse Ringway?"

"Not yet," I lied. "I suppose you haven't any ideas?"

"None at all." He looked over my shoulder. "You'd better go, love. Franks is out looking for you."

I shoved the key in my pocket and ran.

After tea I added a few more things to the stuff in the case—some make-up, tissues, a toothbrush, a hand-towel. Then I changed into mufti. The call came through at exactly half-past six.

I took it in the Home kiosk. It was the same man. "Got the stuff?" he wanted to know.

"Of course."

"That's a good girl. Now, what time can you get out?"

"I can't," I fibbed. "I thought I could maybe leave the case in the front office for you to pick up."

"Tell me another one," he said. "What? And be greeted by a posse of police. How dim do you think I am?"

"Honestly, I swear, I haven't said a single word to the police. Guide's honour."

"I believe you, too. But I'm still not coming to any front office for it, for all that. Can you leave it somewhere outside?"

I thought rapidly, because I was having to adjust my plan. "I could leave it in the rhododendrons, I suppose. They're by the O.P. gate, close to the road. That do?"

"All right. How will I find it?"

"I'll put it right behind the fence, under the bushes, two yards to the left of the gate. It's a yellowish tartan case, you can't miss it."

"Good. Have it there before eight o'clock, will you? And don't hang around looking for me, either. If there's anyone within a hundred yards I shan't pick it up—and you know who'll suffer, don't you?"

"I promise," I said.

When he had rung off I got straight through to the police. Mr. Pallett was out on a case, they said. Would I leave a message? If I did, I reflected, they would be sure to muff it. "No," I told them. "I'll ring again later." Then I rang Sam. He wasn't to be had, either. It looked as if I would have to handle it alone. That suited me. I had it all worked out.

I took the case down to the rhododendron plantation and hid it away tidily. Then I walked round by the road to the other gate and got Simon's car out of the residents' carpark. I drove around the roads for a bit, to get used to it, and at a quarter to eight I went back and parked it at the edge of the ambulance layby, behind the trees. From there I could see the gate, and the bushes but I was pretty in-

visible myself. And even if anyone spotted the outline of the
car it would appear to be waiting for a casualty. I rolled
myself in the rug from the back seat and settled down to
wait, keeping my eyes on the patch of bushes lit by the
gateway lantern.

Simon shook me again. "So this is what you wanted it
for? An *al fresco* snooze. Strange tastes some people do
have."

I sat bolt upright, and stared at him. "Oh, no! What
time is it?"

"Aften ten. I wouldn't have disturbed you, but I thought
you might get locked out."

"Damn," I said. "Damn, damn, *damn*!" Then, obviously,
I had to explain.

When I'd finished he said: "Well. There's a thing. I'd
better nip down and see whether it's gone, hadn't I?"

He came back shaking his head. "No sign of any case.
And somebody's been trampling around down there.
Bigger feet than yours. What does A do now?"

"I certainly can't tell the police, now, can I? I can just
see Detective-sergeant Pallett's face if I told him I'd gone
to sleep on the job."

"What then?"

"Don't think I'm crazy, Simon, but there's something
else . . ." I looked at my watch. "We've got half an hour. It's
really why I borrowed the car. Could we drive up to Hill?
It won't take long." I moved over to let him get into the
driving seat. "It's just a hunch."

"I'm a great believer in following them," he said easily.
"Whereabouts in Hill?"

"The—the new flats, where the farm used to be at the
top of the hill. You know. Something Court."

He turned his head sharply. "Isn't that where——?"

"Yes. It sounds mad, I know, but I've a feeling there's
something wrong. Just drive past, that's all."

We drove slowly past. No lights in the top right-hand

flat, I registered. Then I saw something else. "Simon," I said urgently. "Simon, stop!"

CHAPTER SEVEN

SIMON pulled in obligingly to the kerb. "What now?" he said. "Seen something?"

"Wait," I told him. "There's a girl . . ." I wriggled round to peer through the back window. I had not been mistaken: I could see clearly now in the floodlight shining above the flat entrances. A girl in a University scarf riding a puttering scooter swung out through the gates to overtake us. I gripped Simon's elbow as she buzzed past. "Did you see?"

"That girl? Yes, why? Who is she? It wasn't your friend, was it?"

"Not the girl, you idiot. Get going, Simon. Follow her. Don't you see what's on the carrier? It's the case I left by the rhododendrons." I recognised it easily in the road lights; the garish yellow tartan was unmistakable. "She came out of the flats, didn't you see?"

"She's moving, too." We shot down the hill after the tiny red tail light. "Get us all pinched if she isn't careful. Where do you imagine she's going?"

"She must be on her way to wherever Val is, obviously. All we have to do is to follow her. She must be going *some-where*."

"It may be a long way," Simon pointed out. "You're not suggesting we should keep it up all night, are you?" He leaned nearer the windscreen. "Now where is she?"

"In front of the Hillman," I said. "Oh, Simon, do get a move on!"

He eased his foot down to overtake the car in front. "I'm doing my best. This isn't exactly a speed model, you know. . . . Ah, there she goes."

The girl swung left, away from the main road. I frowned. "She—she can't be going to Thickers, can she?"

"She's going past there, anyway. Unless she's going to jump straight over the cemetery wall. . . . Yes, she's slowing down. What do we do? Roar past and lie in wait, or stalk her?"

"Stalk her," I decided.

Simon switched off his engine and coasted silently down the long hill. Both of us concentrated on the red dot ahead. Then I felt the brakes go on. "She's stopped by the side gate," Simon said. "She's parking the thing by the kerb. If she goes inside we'll give her a moment or two and then follow."

A minute later we picked her up in the headlights. She wasn't going anywhere. She was standing outside the door of the Main Drag, peeping through the glass panel and she had the case in her hand.

I got out of the car as soon as Simon pulled up, and went over to her. "Looking for someone?" I said.

She looked at me, and then at Simon over my shoulder. "Who are you?"

"I work here," I told her. "And that's my case you have there. My name's Brown, if it matters. . . . And this is Dr. James."

She blinked with relief. "Well, thank the lord for that! Here, take the case. It doesn't matter. It was all a stupid rag. I'll explain later. But I've got to get hold of Dr. Cheshire's houseman. Can you——"

"Val isn't hurt, is she? *Where* is she?"

She shrugged. "No idea. On her way back, I expect. That's not important. Can you get him, or can't you?"

"I'll go," Simon offered. "What do I tell him?"

"Just tell him it's terribly important for him to come. It's—it's life and death, actually. I've *got* to see him. Only don't tell anyone else, will you?"

When Simon had gone I turned back to the girl. "Now," I said. "Tell me about Val. What happened to her?"

"Nothing *happened*. Not as far as I know. She's very likely back already. I don't know anything about her. Don't you see, it's far more urgent for me to get hold of this Sam Brown?"

"Sam Brown," I informed her, "happens to be my brother. And we tell one another most things. So suppose you explain?"

She closed her eyes and leaned back against the wall. "When he comes, then." I noticed, then, that she was very pale. She looked as though she'd been missing sleep. I didn't remember ever having seen her before. "Who are you?" I asked her curiously. "You're not one of our students, are you?"

She shook her head. "Mary Coker. My brother's a medical student. Hugh Coker. I'm doing Dip.Ed. myself."

I began to see the light. "I see," I said slowly. "This is all——"

"No, it isn't. Well, it was. It began that way. Only now it isn't funny. Is that him?"

I looked. Sam was jogtrotting down the Main Drag. "Yes. That's Sam."

"Thank God." She meant it, too.

While she talked to him I bobbed inside and left the case under the counter in the front office. When I got back he was saying: "Well, of course I'll come."

"If you're going anywhere," I told him firmly, "I'm coming too. If I get myself shot at dawn for being out late, that's just too bad. Something's happened to Val—I know it has."

"Val?" Sam looked as blank as only Sam can look when it suits him. "*Val?* Not Val, you ass. The Big Cheese!"

My face was suddenly cold. "*What?*"

"Oh, come on, if you're coming. We'll take Simon's car. He said we could. Pile in."

Mary Coker said: "I've got a scooter, down by the——"

"Leave it. This'll be quicker." He didn't know Mary Coker's scooter as I did. "Hop in."

We hopped in. At the Hill flats we hopped out again, and I made for the right-hand entrance. "No, not that way," Mary said. "He's in Partland's flat. Top left. It seemed the obvious place. So easy to get him there, you see, and——"

Sam swerved after her. "And who the hell is Partland?"

"He's a student," I explained, panting after them. "The student to end all students. . . . You wouldn't know. . . . Don't you see, he's the boss of the Rag Committee. He's probably pulling a fast one on you, too, you prize chump. . . . Oh, do wait for me!"

I saw it all now. It was the old ransom game for the Rag fund. It had been done practically every year. One year they'd even kidnapped a film actress they'd inveigled into opening a Carnival Funfair. There had been trouble about that, and they'd been told to lay off. But they never did. Every year Steve Partland—who seemed to have spun out his degree course longer than anyone else—thought up some fresh idiocy. Only it had never entered my head that anyone I knew could be involved. They had been at the dance. They knew where Val was. And what had happened to her. By the time Mary Coker had pushed Sam ahead of her into the Partland flat I was working myself into a fine blaze of annoyance.

I sat down in the small sitting-room and helped myself to a cigarette while I listened to the murmur of voices in the bedroom. There seemed to be too many people in there already, and I needed a moment to calm myself. Mary came out first, with a boy so like her that he had to be her brother. Then Sam followed with Steve Partland. He closed the door carefully behind him. "Phone," he said tersely.

One of them pushed it across to him. Steve Partland—with all the impishness ironed out of his face—said: "Help yourself, old man. You do think——"

"I don't think anything." Sam began to dial. "Except that you're a pack of damn fools. *You* ought to have known better!"

"Well, I tell you, I thought it was malaria. Everybody

knows he gets a burst now and again. He said so himself, confound it. How was I to know?"

Mary sighed. "Shut up, Steve. You're not helping. And I think Hugh and I'd better clear out now." She looked at her brother, and he moved over to the door. "You can ring us. There's nothing we can do now." They got out, fast.

As for me, I waited just long enough to hear Sam say: "You'd better get the consultant-on-call, too. The R.S.O. won't want to be responsible." Then I opened the bedroom door and went in.

He was very ill. There was no question about that. His face had a queer bluish tinge, and though his hands were clammy, his forehead burned my fingers like the bodywork of a car that has stood in strong sunshine all day. He had his eyes closed when I went in, but as soon as I touched him they shot open and stared up at me. There was an insane expression in them, and he clearly didn't know me. "Joy," he said thickly. "Joy . . . don't go away."

"I won't," I promised. So there was somebody. And her name was Joy. I could just imagine her: young, blonde, ineffective. I walked blindly over to the wash-basin in the corner and wrung out a hand-towel in cold water to mop his face. When I had finished I straightened the tossed bedclothes. And all the time he went on muttering about Joy. How kind she was; how gentle; how he could never manage without her; how sorry he was to be such a nuisance to her. If I had to stand in for her I would do it properly, I decided. I said: "Hush, darling. I won't leave you." That was when Sam walked in.

"They're sending the ambulance right away," he said. "God, what a mess! A roaring septicaemia, and those nits thought it was malaria. There'll be the hell of a row over this, you know. You'd better clear out."

I went on holding the restless hand. "Sam, will he do?"

"I don't know. Yes, I suppose so. If we've got him in time. If he doesn't come up with a meningitis or something as well. What a *mess*."

I shivered. "What happened, Sam. Why is he *here*?"

He explained, while we waited for the ambulance. It had been all Steve Partland's idea. That didn't surprise me. They would do one of their regular Carnival kidnap acts, only this time they would snatch a really big fish, they'd decided. But because their victim had fallen sick, they hadn't dared to announce it. He had taken it in good part at first. "Well, he's an Australian," Sam pointed out. "They were banking on his not being stuffy, you see." He hadn't even minded finding himself ambushed when Hugh Coker had told him that Steve Partland had collapsed and would he come at once. Only then he'd begun to feel ill. It was just his malaria, he had told them. He'd felt it coming on for days. "So they gave him a shot of Scotch," Sam said bitterly. "That helped no end, I must say."

When he had finished I said: "But Sam, where's *Val*?"

"How do I know?"

"Well, that girl Mary Coker brought her clothes back. Or the case, anyway. Sam, I'm worried!" It was while I was telling him about the phone calls that I remembered something. "Of course they know. It was Steve Partland who rang me. I knew I'd heard the voice somewhere, only I couldn't place it. It's so long since I saw him. Sam, they've got Val somewhere, too. They must have."

Then we heard the ambulance bell.

I had to go downstairs beside the stretcher, holding his hand, promising not to leave him. The ambulance men thought it was rather funny, I think, but it was just about the least funny thing that ever happened to me. It would have been fine if I hadn't been understudying for Joy, whoever she might be. As it was I felt sick. I didn't even have the mental energy to go back and argue with Steve Partland. When Sam said, "I'll go with him, you bring Simon's crate back," that seemed the easiest thing to do.

It had to be Sister Rhys-Williams who caught me. She shone her torch right into my face under the Hall windows and said: "I might have known! Just what are you doing, Nurse?"

"Trying to get in," I told her frankly. "I'm afraid I'm rather late."

She gave me the usual lecture, to which I didn't even listen, and then added: "That makes two of you for Matron to see in the morning."

I frowned. "Two of us, Sister?"

"You and your friend Nurse Ringway seem to specialise in making nuisances of yourselves, don't you?"

So Val was back. It was a relief, and I suppose I showed it because Sister Rhys-Williams snorted irritably as she let me in through the Home door and reminded me that it was long after lights-out and would I please not imagine that I could spend the rest of the night gossiping. Some people wanted to sleep if I didn't.

I said, "Yes, Sister. Very well, Sister," and bolted up to Val's room.

I scratched at the door and went in to sit on the bed in the dark. "Where on earth have you been?" I said. "We've all been worried stiff."

I heard her sigh. Then she whispered: "What *is* all this? Night Sister made a few odd remarks when I came in. Said I'd had everybody worried, or something. I'm not with it. You might enlighten me." She sat up. "Dash it, I was only ten minutes late."

"Well, where *have* you been?"

"Home, of course. Day off, as usual. I don't see why everybody had to go into a flap just because I'm a few minutes late getting in."

"Day off? Home?" I echoed. "But you said you were having it on Wednesday!"

"So I was. Only when Bulloughs rang through and said——"

"*When?*"

"During the dance, stupid. Didn't she tell you? She had

this interview come up and she wanted me to swop. She fixed it with Sister Thorpe."

"She *can't* have," I pointed out. "She'd have said so when the police——"

Home Sister or no Home Sister, Val reached out then and put on the bedside light. She sat there staring at me. "The *police*? I just don't know what you're talking about!"

"You just went," I said. "No coat, nothing. Nobody knew where you were. You just walked out."

"Oh, that. Yes, well, I did intend to go up and change. Only I left the dance earlier than I meant to—I was a bit wild with Sam, actually—and the Apsley-Hunter Daimler was outside. They'd just brought her back, or something. So old man A-H said if I wanted a lift out his way he'd take me, and I was so wild I just got straight in and went as I was. I knew I'd got plenty of clothes at home to change into, so——"

"Who saw you go?" I said. "Who knew? *Somebody* must have done."

She closed her eyes to think. "Well, there were a fair number of people out there. The Partland gang, and so on. They were up to something, I think, but I don't know what. Yes, because Steve said, 'Have a nice time,' as I went past him."

"So he knew. Then it wasn't Bulloughs who rang you—it can't have been. I'll bet it was Mary Coker."

She opened her eyes wide. "Who the blazes is Mary Coker?"

I explained. "Don't you see," I pointed out. "They *were* up to something. It was *you* they meant to snatch. And you went off with Apsley-Hunter's father under their very noses. . . . So they had to change their plan. *He* came out just after you, and put the idea into their silly little heads."

By the time I'd finished explaining, the whole thing sounded such a muddle that I began to wonder whether I'd dreamed it all.

"Then why did they keep it up, ringing for my clothes and whatnot?" Val wanted to know.

I shook my head. "I've no idea. Using you as a red herring, I suppose, so that nobody would realise they'd got Dr. Cheshire. Or maybe they still hoped to get you. I don't know. I don't know why they do half the things they do." I switched the light out and stood up. "I'm going to bed. My head's reeling."

As I opened the door Val whispered: "You're worried about him, aren't you?"

I didn't answer. "Worried" didn't seem quite the right word, somehow. Besides, I still wanted to know who Joy was.

I felt terrible in the morning. For one thing I'd had hardly any sleep. Anyhow, I couldn't face breakfast. So I took my time getting dressed and went straight down to the front office when I felt mobile enough. The night porter was still there. He said he'd heard my friend had turned up.

"I know," I said. "It was all a mistake. . . . How's Dr. Cheshire. Do you know?"

He grimaced. "Pretty bad, I think. They've had Mr. Lockyer in to him twice. Blood-poisoning, he's got, Mr. Brown said. From that bad finger of his."

"Where is he?"

"Up in Sister Thorpe's side-ward."

"In *Seven*? But that's——"

"Seems there wasn't a surgical bed to be had for love nor money. Anyway, they weren't all that sure which he was, not to be certain. So they put him up in his own ward." He glanced up over my shoulder and turned away. "Yes, Nurse. I'll see it gets posted," he said clearly.

I turned away at once, but not quickly enough to dodge Sister Rhys-Williams. "You again?" she said sharply. "Why were you not at breakfast, Nurse Brown?"

"I overslept, Sister. I'm sorry."

"Quite. *Now* you see why we have rules about the time you go to bed! Matron would like to see you in the office at your coffee-break, please. And see that you're there."

"Yes, Sister."

I was the first on duty in O.P. I still hadn't got myself organised when Peter Stead came through from Casualty, stripping off a rubber apron. "Why is it," he wanted to know, "that people always fall off their bicycles going to work, and never going home?"

I said it was probably psychological. "People don't often prevent themselves from going to places they want to go to. Maybe they don't want to go to work?"

I waited for him to say something about Dr. Cheshire, and he didn't let me down. "Rough about the old Cheese. I suppose you heard?"

"Oh, yes, I heard," I agreed. "Actually, I was there. I went along with Sam last night."

"You did?" His eyes widened. "You get around, don't you, sweetie?"

"How is he, Peter? Will he do?"

Peter shrugged, and began to scrub his hands. "Should do. But you never know, do you? Hell of an infection, they say. I suppose it invaded through his finger."

That reminded me of something. I said: "I'm horribly afraid I was the last to dress it. But I'm sure I didn't——"

"Sucks!" Peter said. "Not your fault. He mucked about with it in the first place, and it never really had a chance to quieten down. You know him: he isn't capable of resting it."

I changed the subject. "Val's back."

"She is? Don't tell me she was with him too?"

"No, it was—she thought it was her day off. No mystery."

"Do you mean to tell me we had all those policemen and things here and she was at home all the time? Didn't they get in touch with her people?"

"Apparently not. Mind you, they're not on the phone, and they've only just moved in, so——"

"I should have thought the very first thing Matron would do would be to contact them."

I sighed. "Matron wouldn't. Don't you see? She's a bit of a one, but she'd leave it a day before she did that. She wouldn't want to put Val in bad with her folks if it was just what she'd call a 'prank'."

Peter reached for the towel I was holding ready for him and contrived to hold my hand underneath it. "Well, it's over now. . . . Cheer up, Brownie! Nobody's going to shoot you."

"Aren't they?" I jerked my hand away. "I've to see Matron at nine o'clock. Maybe she will. Maybe she'll throw me out altogether, this time."

"What have you done now?"

"Nothing much. Came in late. I couldn't very well clear off until the ambulance came, could I?"

"What could be simpler than explaining just that?" He tossed the towel back to me. "Simply tell her where you were."

I felt like telling him that I didn't want anyone to know. Nor did I want anyone to know that I'd been crazy enough to go round worrying about a man who couldn't even see me, who had looked at me unseeingly and called me "Joy" and asked me not to leave him. "Maybe I will," I agreed. But I knew that I never should.

"And then come out with Uncle Peter tonight, and tell him all about it, huh?"

"Why not?" I said, thinking aloud.

He came over to me and took both my hands in his damp clean ones. "I meant it," he said gently.

"I know." This time I left my wrists where they were and didn't pull back. "Yes, I'll come out with you. Where shall we go?"

He let his palms slip up to my elbows. "You're getting thin, Brownie. I'll take you out and feed you, shall I?"

"You do that. I'll be ready around seven, if I don't have to stay on late as a penance," I promised.

Staff Williams stalked in between us at that point and told me to go over and help with dressings until nine o'clock. "And at nine," her look said, "don't forget you'll be seeing Matron."

All the time I was bandaging and strapping, cleaning, probing and pouring out lotions I was telling myself I must have been mad. Peter wasn't interested in me, and I wasn't interested in Peter. There wasn't much point in starting that all over again. Staff Timmins teased me about being pre-occupied, and when she had gone out Mr. Birch said: "I've been in love myself. I quite understand. But it was a two-inch bandage I asked you for, Nurse dear."

"I'm sorry," I said. "I'm not in love, anyway. I'm just tired."

He grinned. "Rubbish. Of course you are. All girls are at your age. Something wrong with you if you're not." He finished off the otitis child he was dressing, and sent him back to his mother in the ante-room, and then he turned his back to me while he scrubbed. "I know you are. But I'm not quite sure who with."

"Neither am I," I confessed. "There at least we see eye to eye. Do you want to see that old osteo who's waiting outside?"

"Not in the least. But I shall have to. I think we'll probably have to admit him. There's a sequestrum there as big as the Matron's left foot, if I'm any judge."

"Cheating, Mr. Birch. You've seen the pictures."

"Are they up?"

"They're on the projector."

"Good girl." He walked over to look, drying his hands as he went. "Oh, yes. My goodness, yes. A beauty. He'll have to come in."

"Today?"

"No sense in cooking it, is there?"

"I suppose not. Only I don't think there are likely to be any surgical beds. At least, there weren't last night when——" I stopped and blushed. "I mean——"

He beamed. "I see. *Now* I see. Yes. Most unsuitable, but understandable. Well, well, well. Thank you, Nurse—bring this chap in, will you? And then ring up and see about the bed."

I was glad to walk out.

I had to wait a long time to get into the office. And it evidently wasn't Matron's morning, because half the people who came out ahead of me looked as though they'd been crying. By the time she called me in life seemed hardly worth living. I found her surrounded by Change lists and looking thoroughly disorganised. She let me stand there for a minute or two before she looked up, and then she said: "Ah, Nurse Brown. Yes. Sit down, Nurse."

That was bad. Matron didn't ask people to sit down unless she had bad news. Or unless they had done something absolutely frightful. It was her way of getting a captive audience, as it were. I sat down abruptly, waiting for it. "Yes, Matron?" I said.

She fished out one of the lists and peered at it. "Yes. I expect you know that we're putting the Change forward by a week? It's so that we can fit in three extra study days. I dare say Sister Tutor explained to you."

Sister Tutor had done nothing of the sort, but I said: "Yes, Matron."

"Yes. Well, you'll be going to nights, this time, of course. Now Sister Mumby has asked me whether you can go to Seven. On the female side. But I'm not sure that it would be wise. I understand now, of course, about your brother. Why you didn't explain yourself I really can't understand. All the same . . . Do you think you can manage up there?"

For the third time I said: "Yes, Matron."

"Hm. You really ought to go to the theatre, this Change. But I can't fit it in yet. . . . Very well, Nurse. I shall put you down as senior in Seven. You'll go on tomorrow night, then."

I couldn't make the same remark for a fourth time, and

as she evidently had no intention of saying anything about my lateness the previous night I ventured to ask: "Who will be my junior, then, Matron?"

"Let me see . . . one of the current day people, of course. Yes. Nurse Luck. You're fairly close together in seniority, so I hope you'll work well together."

I couldn't have been more pleased. I said: "I'm sure we shall, Matron." I stood up to leave. "Is that all, Matron?"

"Not quite, Nurse. I hear you were reprimanded last night by Night Sister for coming in late?"

I said it again.

"Well, I've explained to Sister Rhys-Williams that you were out on an 'errand of mercy', as we say." Unexpectedly she bared her teeth in a smile. "So we'll forget about it. Incidentally, I'm very glad to hear that Nurse Ringway's absence has been explained. Some student prank, I gather. I'm sure Nurse didn't willingly cause us so much anxiety."

I said, "No, Matron," by way of a change, and then, "Thank you, Matron," before I closed the door.

When I got back to O.P. the telephone was ringing. I picked it up as I passed, and because my mouth was still half full of the bun I had snatched from the canteen in mid-flight I suppose my voice sounded a little odd. Someone—a man—said: "Is that you, Joy?"

I swallowed, and then said incoherently that it wasn't, but I'd get her. Then I left the receiver dangling while I got hold of Middleman. I said. "Who the heck is 'Joy'?"

She grinned. "Staff Williams, I suppose."

"But her name isn't Joy. She signs herself——"

"I know. It's what He calls her."

"Who, for Pete's sake?"

"How do I know? Some man who rings her up. So I'm told. Why?"

I would have liked to tell her why, but she wouldn't have understood. And since Staff Williams seemed to have gone to the canteen, I took great pleasure in going back to the telephone and putting on a sort of admin voice to tell the caller that she wasn't available, and that nurses were not expected to receive personal calls while on duty.

"Not even from her cousin?" he said.

"No. Not even from her brother," I told him firmly. Then I put the receiver down sharply.

I didn't see Val until lunchtime, and then she was at the other side of the table. She shook her head, and mouthed: "He's not doing too well."

That just about made my day.

All through Dr. Sweeney's clinic I tried to cheer myself up by thinking about Peter Stead, and the fact that we were going out for a meal, but it didn't really work. And when they phoned through from Seven to ask whether we'd seen Mr. Lockyer, because they wanted him up there, I knew I'd been a complete fool to agree to go out at all.

CHAPTER EIGHT

I FINALLY got hold of Val after duty, around six o'clock, when she was racing to bag a bathroom, unfastening her collar as she went. "Hold hard," I said. "I haven't had a single minute to talk to you since——"

"Can't stop." She grinned. "The lord and master awaits."

"You're going out with Sam?" I panted alongside. "But I want to ask you about Dr. Cheshire. Val, wait!"

She stopped then. "Of course. So sorry, I meant to tell you. He's had no end of antibiotics and stuff, and he's just the weeniest bit better. Well, Mr. Lockyer reckons he is—he looks ghastly to me."

She simply wasn't interested. I said: "You just don't care, do you, Val? All you think about is your precious Sam. I do think you might——"

"Of course I'm not interested . . . Oh, *lord*! You are. You really are, aren't you? Look, I'm sorry. But why you had to fall for him I shall never know." She sounded impatient.

I thought of the time I had danced with him, out in the moonlight. And then I dragged in a deep breath and remembered his voice saying: "Joy . . . don't leave me." The sick feeling came back. "No, I'm not interested," I told her. "I haven't fallen for him. Not the way you mean."

"No? And you could have Peter toeing the line any time you wanted. But you'd rather waste yourself on——"

"On somebody who can't even see me? You must think I'm dim, Val. As a matter of fact, I'm going out with Peter tonight. For a meal, or something."

That pleased her. "And very sensible, too. Look, I've got to go. I can't keep Sam waiting."

I let her go. I was disappointed in Val. She had changed completely. And what she saw in Sam I couldn't imagine. He hadn't been in the least perturbed when she was missing, I reflected. And if he stuck to her—to any girl—it would be the first time. I knew my Sam, and he wasn't the steady kind, I told myself. He was just another Peter Stead. . . .

Three hours later I sat in Peter's car, in Peter's arms, on the edge of Middleton Woods, and thought again. He was saying: "Let's face it, lovey, it *is* time I settled down. Isn't it?"

"Settled down?" I said obtusely. I moved a little closer to him and put my head under his chin. "How d'you mean?"

"Sweet, I've been telling you. . . . I get so involved. And I don't mean to. But you know how it is. . . . I'll get promotion any minute now, and I could just about afford to be a respectable married man. Well, with a strong-minded wife to watch over me, you know."

"I'm not a bit strong minded," I said. "You'd better marry Sister Rhys-Williams. *She'd* manage you all right."

"Darling, please! I don't want to be managed. I just want to be loved. And you do, just a little bit, don't you?"

"Do I?" I sighed. "Honestly, Peter, I don't know. There are times when I think so, and then there are times when I don't. When I'm with you there isn't anyone else. But when I'm not . . ."

"Then stay with me. Simple. Brownie, it's at least five minutes since I kissed you. I can't bear it."

I knew then that it was high time I grew up, and stopped dreaming childish dreams. "No," I said. "I don't think I can, either. I do love you really, Peter. It's just that I can't get used to saying so."

"Then show me." He lifted my chin and kissed me very gently. As always it was like old times. The next was different—much more possessive—and we were both a little breathless when he let me go. My eyes were wet, too. I said: "I suppose we shall have to tell people, shan't we?"

"Don't you want to, sweet?"

I shook my head under his chin. "Not just yet. Only Val and Sam, anyway."

"I shan't be able to bottle it up for long. Not more than one day, anyhow. Besides, we've got to get a ring, and all that. Haven't we?"

It all sounded so final, and I was afraid. "Must we?"

Peter shouted with laughter and a startled bird squawked in the bushes beside the car. "I thought all girls were mad keen to get this ring and wear it, and show it to their chums. That's what my mother taught me. Of course we must. What's it to be? Do you have a birthstone, or something? Or shall we be all traditional and make it a solitaire diamond? Or what?"

I thought about it carefully. Or as carefully as I could with Peter's heart thudding so close to my ear and his mouth in my hair. Then I said: "Amethyst, please."

"An odd choice, my love. Surely that's only semi-precious, isn't it?"

"Then it's like me," I said. "I'm not used to being valued. At any rate, it's supposed to protect from drunkenness and evil passions."

That made him laugh. "Are those your besetting sins, my sweet? I must say I never suspected it."

"Oh, yes. Especially evil passions. . . . I've been an awful fool, Peter. . . . I get carried away, you know. You'll have to keep me on a tight rein."

"I'll have to hire a few colourful eunuchs with whacking great knives to watch over you. And a couple of Alsatians. That ought to do the trick. Or lock you up like Rapunzel. You haven't much hair to let down, so you'd be quite safe."

"But awfully bored," I pointed out. "Shan't you let me go on working?"

"Certainly not. What? Expose you to all the hazards of Thickers? Especially by night."

I kissed his jawline gently. "That reminds me. I go on nights tomorrow. In Seven of all places. Sister Mumby must be fonder of me than I knew. She actually *asked* for me."

"Why are you always so surprised when anyone appreciates you, darling? It's very refreshing, but quite unnecessary." He tightened his arms. "But I shall never see you, if you're back in Seven."

"You will," I promised. "But you'll have to let me go on until I've taken my Final State, Peter. Only a year and a bit."

"I'll think about that. But I'd much rather you didn't."

The next time I came up for air I said irrelevantly: "I didn't know Staff Williams was called 'Joy', did you?"

"I understand it's what she *likes* to be called. By the boys, you know. But I can't say it suits her. Why?"

"Nothing. I just wondered." I shivered suddenly. "We must go, Peter. It's getting cold out here. And I know I'm going to be late again."

"So? I can hoist you through a window." He took his arm away reluctantly. "When do we go shopping for this ring?"

"Tomorrow afternoon," I said firmly. "If we have to do it we'd better get it over. I don't suppose I shall believe I'm engaged until I have it."

"Nor will anyone else. And if it's to protect you from

evil passions and all the rest of it, the sooner you're protected the better I shall be pleased. All right. Tomorrow afternoon. I could get out from two till four if I talk nicely to old Birch."

I thought of my last conversation with Mr. Birch. "Shall you tell him why?"

"Probably. Do you mind?"

"No," I said. "Not really. As a matter of fact, you can tell him that I specially wanted him to know. He was teasing me last time I saw him."

"Oh? About what?"

"He said I was in love."

"Was he right, sweet?"

"What do you think?"

We didn't finish the conversation. Not in words, anyhow.

I went on duty the next night wearing Peter's amethyst round my neck on a thin gold chain. He bought the chain specially. "I'm a man of the world," he said. "*I* know where nurses wear their rings when they're on duty."

"They usually wear them strung on bits of bandage," I said. "That's what most of the girls do."

"Not my girl," Peter said possessively. "We of the Stead family do things in style. . . . That reminds me: you'll have to come and vet the family one evening. When you get nights off."

"You mean they'll vet me. Will they approve, Peter?"

"They'd better! They'll be shot to pieces at the idea of their mad son settling down, though. You must tell them I've reformed."

"Have you?"

"There are those who will think so. Including your Sam. I haven't told him yet. Have you?"

"Not yet. I'm waiting to see Val, first. To flash my ring at her, you know."

In fact, Val flashed first. We met briefly in the Bunny Run as I went on duty, and she dragged me into the auxiliaries' cloakroom and fumbled under her apron bib. "Look," she said. "What do you know about that?"

Hers was an aquamarine, but I pulled mine out too and said: "Snap!"

There was only time to hug one another and grin before I hurried on, and I didn't ask any questions. But when Staff Horrocks had finished giving me the report and taken herself off I went into the kitchen, where Kerry Luck was checking off her drinks list. "Who's on the male side?" I said. "I didn't have a second to look at the notice-board."

"Our Pirie, Nurse. Seems she's done hardly any male stuff at all. So they slung her across there. I don't know who her junior is. Some dim little thing with no chin. The girls call her Mouse, so you know the kind. Why?"

"Because I'm just nipping across for a minute, before Sister rears her ugly head," I explained. "If she comes, drop something in the corridor to tip me off, will you?"

She opened her eyes. "Such as what?"

"Something tinkly. A spoon, or something. Then head her off into the side-ward while I shoot over. All right?"

"All right," she nodded. "I'll do that thing."

Pirie came out of the ward kitchen as soon as she heard me. She isn't the kind you have to waste words on. She jerked her head for me to follow her into the side-ward next to the linen-room and went round the screens. "You can come in," she murmured. "He's asleep."

He still looked quite dreadful. But he was better, I could see that. Better, but still horribly flat. I moved into the little circle of dim light and touched his wrist. Not for any other reason than because I wanted to be sure that the contact meant nothing to me. And then Kerry Luck did her drop-ping act. It wasn't a spoon, but something that sounded like a whole trayful of them, and I could hear Sister Rhys-Williams grumbling as I shot towards the door, not looking where I was going. By the time I had disentangled myself from the screen and chased across the flat to the female side I realised that I had probably disturbed Dr. Cheshire, but it wasn't the moment to stay and apologise to Pirie. She would understand.

"She's gone," Kerry Luck told me. "She said she wasn't doing her round, yet. She just wanted to get through to the garden. God knows what for. Maybe she has some sort of assignation? You should have heard her when I dropped the drinks tray."

"Was that what it was? It sounded like Thermopylae in full belt."

"Well, I'd just picked it up, and I had it in my hand, and there wasn't time to get a spoon. So I thought I'd better drop that. She fairly blistered me."

"Bless you," I said. "I'll do the same for you some time. Now let's get on with it. She'll be back in no time at all, you'll see."

In fact, she didn't arrive until I rang for her when Mr. Franks did his round at eleven. When he had gone she settled down at the table and went through the report comparatively amiably. I was surprised. Then she looked up inquisitively and said: "I hear you're engaged to Mr. Stead, Nurse. Is it true?"

I wondered who had told her. But news travels so fast in hospital that I wasn't really surprised. "Yes, Sister," I said. "Today, actually."

"I see. Congratulations." She was waiting for something. "Well?"

I wasn't used to the game, yet. "Of course," I said. "You might like to see my ring." I put two fingers between my dress buttons under my apron bib. Then I patted myself. Finally, I wriggled. The ring simply wasn't there. "It's gone," I told her feebly. "I must have dropped it somewhere." I looked wildly round the ward floor. "I hope nobody steps on it."

Sister Rhys-Williams sighed with exasperation. "Really, Nurse Brown! Why *are* you so careless? You'd better get Nurse Luck to help you to look for it at once. And then get

these light dimmed. It's very late to be finishing up. . . .
What sort of ring is it?"

"Amethyst," I told her abstractedly. "Amethyst, Sister.
With little diamonds round the edge, you know."

Her eyebrows went up. "Really? How very unlucky!
Not a stone I'd choose myself, I must say." That was
entirely typical. I'd thought all along it was too good to be
true that she could appear to be doing a round without a
single catty remark.

Kerry Luck said: "No use looking until you've thought.
Where are you *sure* you last had it?"

"Breakfast," I remembered. "Chapel . . . yes, and I had
it when——" I had touched it through my uniform, I knew,
as I'd walked over to the female side. "I had it when I went
over to—to see Pirie."

"Maybe you dropped it over there? Think."

I nodded. "Yes. I'll bet I know when it happened, too. I
nearly climbed up a screen when you dropped that tray."

"Shall I run over?"

"No. No, we can't go chasing about the place with Sister
buzzing around. I'll give Pirie a ring."

But before I could pick up the receiver the phone rang.
The Casualty girl said: "I know it isn't strictly your take-
in until midnight, but I can't fix a bed anywhere else. Five
are stacked. All right?"

"What is it?"

"Pneumonia. An old girl they picked up sleeping rough.
Pretty messy."

I sighed. "All right. It'll be near enough midnight by the
time we've admitted her. I suppose Sister knows?"

"She knows, chum. She's down here herself."

"Well, I love the way you *ask* me! I suppose she's telling
me to take it, actually? Right. Send it up. Give me a few
minutes, will you? I'll have to lug up the oxygen and whatnot."

Casualty's "pretty messy" was something of an under-
statement. The old dear was caked with dirt. She didn't

smell exactly glamorous, either. Kerry Luck wrinkled her nose. "Why is it always the night people who get them?"

"Not to worry," I told her. "She's much too ill to wash. Bung her between a couple of bath blankets for now and we'll clean her up later, when they've pushed their shots into her. Get the oxygen started right away. I expect Mr. Franks will be up. Or Sam."

In fact, it was Sam. We stood together looking down at the blue face and the painfully working nostrils, listening to the grunting respiration, after he'd shot in penicillin and written up a whole lot of stuff that I knew the old woman would never get. "Do you think she'll do, Sis?" he said superfluously.

"I hate saying 'no'," I said, "but that's how it feels to me. What chance have you got when they come in like this? It isn't your fault, Sam."

"Oh, well . . ." He stood there brooding over the end of the bed. "I'd have liked to do something. But I'm no miracle-man."

To cheer him up I said: "By the way—congratulations. You didn't tell me this was coming off."

"No. Well, I didn't know myself until it happened, as you might say."

"I've been and gone and done the same thing myself."

His face lit up, and he turned away from the bed. "You have? Well, good old Sis! Do I ask who's the victim?"

"I'll leave you to work that out for yourself. Hush, Sister's here again." I went forward to meet her.

She had her niggly expression well on this time, and I knew why as soon as she opened her outstretched hand. "I found *this* in the male-side side-ward, Nurse Brown. I presume it's yours?"

I said it was, and took it from her.

"Well? How do you account for its being over there?"

Sam, craning over the screen, saved me. "Sister—can you come here a second?"

She glared at me as she went. A few minutes later he

walked her out of the ward, talking all the way. There are times when a brother comes in useful.

Pirie's junior walked along to Meal with me at midnight. She said: "I've got a message for you from Nurse Pirie. She found a ring in the side-ward, and she thought it might be yours. An amethyst. She says will you collect it, if it is."

"It is," I told her. "And I already have it. Sister brought it over."

"Did she?" She frowned. "That's funny. We left it on the side-ward bed-table in case you came across. How did *she* know it was yours?"

"This must be your first night-duty, Nurse," I said. "By the time you've been on a bit longer you'll realise that night sisters know just about everything that goes on. And what they don't know they make up. So beware."

There wasn't a single buddy of mine on nights, except Pirie, and she would never be at the same Meal. It was the first time Val and I had been parted, and I missed her. At this hour it didn't seem such a bad idea, after all, to throw in my hand and get married without finishing my training. There wasn't even anyone to tell about that, so I ploughed through the cottage pie and stewed fruit as quickly as I could and went back to the ward. Luck would probably be getting anxious about the pneumonia woman, anyway.

She met me on the corridor outside the ward, looking shaken. I said: "Has she gone?"

She nodded. "There just wasn't anything I could do, was there? Or was there?"

"Not a thing," I assured her. "Just ring for Mr. Brown, and tell Sister, will you?" I went along to make sure, and moved all the paraphernalia out of the way. For the first time I looked properly at the case-sheet Luck had made out. *Martha Todd, aged 87*, it read. *No fixed address*. It seemed a poor cheap way to finish. I told myself not to be sentimental; that if we'd managed to keep her there would have been no comfortable future. The best she could have expected was a bare bed in a drab room in an old folks' home, with no privacy or independence. At least she wouldn't have to face that.

Kerry Luck came to help me when Sam had been and gone. Together we made Martha Todd clean and sweet for the first time in years, and folded her in a clean white sheet. "Imagine it," Luck murmured. "Eighty-seven, and sleeping rough. Poor old scrap." She went into the bathroom and came back with a spray of white lilac. "Here," she said. "It must be long enough since she had any flowers." She slipped it between the thin blue fingers and folded the sheet across them. She was a nice girl.

Things were pretty rushed from then on, and I was glad not to have much time for thinking, because I wasn't feeling exactly clear-headed. The small hours of the morning are odd that way: every night nurse takes mighty decisions at three in the morning and wonders by eight what could have possessed her. In my case it was not so much a matter of taking a decision as of undoing one, and it seemed best to keep busy.

I still felt woolly and confused when I went off duty in the morning. So when Sister Mumby said: "Just you go straight to bed, Nurse Brown. You look half dead!" I was quite happy to oblige. I didn't even go in to dinner.

Looking back, now, I suppose it must have been something like a week or ten days before I stopped feeling like that. I went through the routine in a weary daze, said, "Yes, Sister," and, "No, Sister," and dealt with the patients, without letting my own private thoughts come up for air at all. And then one night Staff Timmins bustled in. "Sister's nights-off," she announced. "So let's not have any insurrection. How are you, Nurse Brown? I haven't seen you for ages."

"All right," I said. "I think. At least, I'm a bit tired. I don't think I've adjusted yet."

"To what? Night-duty? Or being engaged?"

"Both," I said. "And if this is being engaged I don't think much of it. I haven't seen Peter ever since I came on, except to wave to."

She waited until Kerry Luck had walked past, and then she murmured: "I never thought you would, you know."

"Would what, Staff?"

"Get yourself engaged to Mr. Stead. You always gave me the impression that—— Well, never mind. It's not my business. I'd better look at the report and go round, I suppose."

We got down to business. She took the report, went round, glanced at the four-hourly charts, checked the sedatives and noted the enquiry changes in a quarter of the time it would have taken Sister Rhys-Williams. Not until I was seeing her out did she say: "By the way, Dr. Cheshire seems a good deal better. I do wish he'd get more sleep, though."

"Doesn't he?"

"No, he's very restless. Have you been to see him?"

"Me? No! Not since first night on—I peeped in at him then."

She tapped my forearm, not looking at me. "I should if I were you. Pop in on your way to Meal. You do that."

It seemed a remarkable thing for her to say. I couldn't imagine what was in her mind. "Heavens," I said. "He'd hardly want to see *me*."

"That," she said, "is what you think. Aunt Timmins knows better. Do as you're told, Nurse. I told you I wanted no insurrection tonight, didn't I?" She walked away smiling to herself.

When I did make myself go across the flat Pirie said: "And about time, too. I told Staff Timmins to tell you he was asking for you. He's in a fine state. For Pete's sake go on in and quieten him, then perhaps we'll all get some peace."

"Asking for *me*?" I stared at her. "You out of your mind, or something? Nights has a queer effect on some people, you know. They see things that aren't there, and hear things that aren't said. Night nurses' paralysis, or something of the sort."

"Pish," she said. "Go on in, do. And close the door behind you."

I went in. I also closed the door behind me. Then I walked round the screen to the bed. He was propped up, and his eyes were wide open. There was a little colour in his cheeks, too. I said awkwardly: "You look much better."

He held out both hands. "Joy," he said. "You've come. You've really come."

This time he wasn't delirious, I was pretty sure. I stayed where I was and said: "My name isn't Joy."

"In my mind it's never been anything else. Ever since the night I first heard you singing."

I moved closer. It was all a kind of dream, I knew that, but I had to take my cue the way one does in dreams. "Singing? But I *can't* sing."

He closed his eyes. "You were up in Ward Seven, and you were singing something about 'Joy, joy joy, there's a song of joy for you'. And it fitted you. You are joy yourself. To me, anyway. Come here." His eyes opened again and he took my right hand in both his. "I've told Nurse Pirie I shan't go to sleep until I've seen you, and asked you just one question."

I began to tremble. "No. You mustn't. Please."

"Dearest, I must. It's quite simple. Have you ever read Freud's *Psychopathology of Everyday Life*?"

That was so totally unexpected that I very nearly laughed with relief. "Of course. It's a set book."

"Then tell me about people who lose things."

"They—they lose things they don't want, obviously."

"And if they lose valuable things?"

"They don't value them." Then I saw where this was leading "But that's different," I protested. "It was an accident. It was because I——"

"All right. I don't think you'll lie to me. People hardly ever do. . . . Look at me."

I looked, and I was dazzled by his eyes.

"Now," he said. "Go on looking at me, and tell me that you value the ring you dropped in here. Tell me that Peter Stead is the man you want to spend the rest of your life with. Go on. *Tell* me."

My voice came out in a kind of cracked whisper. "You can't do this to me," I said wildly. "You *mustn't*. It's—— I'm engaged to Peter."

"*Tell* me."

When I began to cry he let me go. I walked blindly out and stumbled into the kitchen. Pirie, sitting on the table with a cup of tea in her hand, said: "Well? Have you straightened him out?"

I mopped my face with cold water at the sink, and then I said: "It's I who need straightening out."

"Well, you know what to do."

"Yes," I agreed. "I know what to do. Only I don't know how to do it."

"Well . . . there's the phone. Or you could write it. Or you could see him."

I looked at her hard. "How do you know so much about me?"

"Dear girl, everybody knows everything about everybody in this place, let's face it. And I have had the added advantage of hearing just what our friend next door feels about you. You've made a bit of a bloomer, but it's not too late to put it right. These things do happen. . . . Actually, I don't think Peter Stead's going to take it very hard. He isn't the type. I'd like to bet he's wondering already what on earth made him ruin a beautiful friendship by tying himself up."

"It *is* a good friendship," I told her defensively.

"But of course! You know one another well. You can say most things to one another. You'll even be able to say this to him. You'll see. He's a good-tempered type."

I knew she was right. And that Peter and I would always be close. Only not that close. After I'd drunk the tea she poured for me I said: "I'd better go and tell——" I stopped. "I don't even know his first name. Isn't that silly?"

"It's John," he told me, five minutes later. "Very ordinary. I still don't know yours, and I don't care, because I shall always call you Joy."

"I hate it. It's Jocelyn. But everybody calls me Brownie."

"Have you decided?"

I nodded. I was still ashamed of the muddle I'd made. "I shall tell him as soon as I can. Until then——"

"Until then, my darling, I shan't poach on his preserves. I shan't even ask you whether you'll have me. But I love you more than I can say. Is that enough?" He smiled, and began to sing softly: *"He loves thee, he is here . . ."*

"That was when I really knew," I said. "At that concert." I dimmed his light. "Will you sleep now, John?"

"Yes, my darling. I shall sleep." He closed his eyes.

It wasn't really cheating. My decision was already made. I bent down and kissed him very gently on the lips. Then I went back across the flat and got on with my work. There was so much to get through before morning. And in the morning my whole life would fall neatly into place. I was singing again as I did my early washings.

Mrs. Andrews—who scarcely looked like an Addison's any more—said: "You sound so happy, Nurse. What are you thinking about?"

"I can only tell you part of it." I folded her towel neatly while I thought it out. "Partly I was thinking about a poor old soul named Martha Todd, and being glad I'm not alone in the world. Partly . . . well, the sun's shining."

"And that's all we're going to know, hm?"

"That's right," I said. "That's all you're going to know." I couldn't possibly have put the rest of it into words in any case.

THE END

A SELECTION OF FINE READING
AVAILABLE IN CORGI BOOKS

NOVELS

☐ FN1467	A WALK ON THE SIDE	Nelson Algren	5/–
☐ GN1311	GO TELL IT ON THE MOUNTAIN	James Baldwin	3/6
☐ SN1373	GIOVANNI'S ROOM	James Baldwin	2/6
☐ GN1514	THE TWO SISTERS	H. E. Bates	3/6
☐ GN1520	THE PASSION OF GABRIELLE	Malcolm Stuart Boylan	3/6
☐ GN7002	MIGNON	James M. Cain	3/6
☐ FN1278	THE GINGER MAN	J. P. Donleavy	5/–
☐ FN1100	THE INTERNS	Richard Frede	5/–
☐ FN1256	THE SONS AND THE DAUGHTERS	Patricia Gallagher	5/–
☐ FN1502	THE COBWEB	William Gibson	5/–
☐ FN1466	DIAMOND	Brian Glanville	5/–
☐ FN1500	CATCH-22	Joseph Heller	5/–
☐ FN1485	CROSSWIND	Robert Henry	5/–
☐ EN1516	SOW NOT IN ANGER	Jack Hoffenberg	7/6
☐ XN1200	MOTHERS AND DAUGHTERS	Evan Hunter	6/–
☐ FN1489	STRANGERS WHEN WE MEET	Evan Hunter	5/–
☐ GN1410	THE PHILANDERER	Stanley Kauffman	3/6
☐ FN1455	SEVEN DAYS IN MAY	Knebel and Bailey	5/–
☐ FN1533	COMPULSION	Meyer Levin	5/–
☐ FN1394	THIS IS MY STREET	Nan Maynard	5/–
☐ GN1505	NO MEAN CITY	McArthur and Long	3/6
☐ FN7001	TALES OF THE SOUTH PACIFIC	James A. Michener	5/–
☐ FN1066	LOLITA	Vladimir Nabokov	5/–
☐ FN1393	SERMONS AND SODA-WATER	John O'Hara	5/–
☐ FN1484	ASSEMBLY	John O'Hara	5/–
☐ SN1486	BENIGHTED	J. B. Priestley	2/6
☐ GN1519	THE SHAPES OF SLEEP	J. B. Priestley	3/6
☐ FN1162	A STONE FOR DANNY FISHER	Harold Robbins	5/–
☐ FN1187	79 PARK AVENUE	Harold Robbins	5/–
☐ FN1202	NEVER LOVE A STRANGER	Harold Robbins	5/–
☐ SN1204	NEVER LEAVE ME	Harold Robbins	2/6
☐ EN1440	UHURU	Robert Ruark	7/6
☐ EN1441	POOR NO MORE	Robert Ruark	7/6
☐ XN1517	THE LIFE OF AN AMOROUS WOMAN	Ihara Saikaku	6/–
☐ FN1487	THE DOCTORS	André Soubiran	5/–
☐ FN1133	THE CARETAKERS	Dariel Telfer	5/–
☐ FN1355	MILA 18	Leon Uris	5/–
☐ FN1515	TO LOVE AND CORRUPT	Joseph Viertel	5/–
☐ FN1532	THE WILD SUMMER	Jack Wilson	5/–
☐ GN474	FOREVER AMBER (Vol. One)	Kathleen Winsor	3/6
☐ GN475	FOREVER AMBER (Vol. Two)	Kathleen Winsor	3/6

WAR

☐ FB1490	THE CRUMBLING FORTRESS	Willi Heinrich	5/–
☐ FB1521	THE DEAD, THE DYING AND THE DAMNED	D. J. Hollands	5/–
☐ GB1461	THREE CAME HOME	Agnes Keith	3/6
☐ SB1506	THE MAN WHO NEVER WAS	Ewen Montagu	2/6
☐ GB1148	MEDICAL BLOCK: BUCHENWALD	Walter Poller	3/6
☐ GB1472	THE SCOURGE OF THE SWASTIKA	Lord Russell of Liverpool	3/6
☐ GB1473	THE KNIGHTS OF BUSHIDO	Lord Russell of Liverpool	3/6
☐ FB1183	THE DEATHMAKERS	Glen Sire	5/–
☐ GB1535	633 SQUADRON	Frederick E. Smith	3/6
☐ FB1499	FACTORY OF DEATH	Vrba and Bestic	5/–

ROMANCE

☐ GR1511	QUEEN SHE	Victoria Farlow	3/6
☐ SR1525	LARKSBROOK	Margaret Maddocks	2/6
☐ SR1539	HOUSEMAN'S SISTER	Hilary Neal	2/6